SILVER SERIES

SUPERB WRITING
TO FIRE THE IMAGINATION

Susan Price won the Guardian Award for *The Sterkarm Handshake* in 1999 and the Carnegie Medal for *Ghost Drum* in 1987. Her story collections: *Hauntings*, *Nightcomers*, *The Story Collector* and *Telling Tales*, are all published by Hodder in Signature.

Susan Price writes, 'I had agreed to write a fantasy novel for Hodder, but didn't yet know what it would be. I was on the dance-floor with my bloke, when the DJ put on that old record, the one that goes: "We are fam-i-lee: I've got all my sisters with me." Immediately, the idea of the Wolf-Sisters leaped into my mind. Later, when I wondered what their story would be, I found that it was all there, already in my head. My subconscious had obviously been hard at work. It isn't often as easy to come up with a book but, with *The Wolf Sisters*, I was lucky.'

Praise for *The Wolf Sisters*: 'Beautifully crafted . . . Drawn into the action, totally convinced of the reality of the characters, readers should not miss this fantasy.' *Carousel*.

†HE WOLF-SiSTERS

SUSAN PRICE

Hodder
Children's
Books

a division of Hodder Headline Limited

This paperback edition first published in Great Britain in 2001
as part of Hodder Silver Series
by Hodder Children's Books

www.susanprice.org.uk

A Catalogue record for this book is available from the British Library

ISBN 0 340 80544 7

Typeset by Avon Dataset Ltd, Bidford-on-Avon, Warks

Printed and bound in Great Britain by
Clays Ltd, St Ives plc

Hodder Children's Books
a division of Hodder Headline Limited
338 Euston Road
London NW1 3BH

1

The traveller

The door-keeper left his small hut, shivering in the cold night, and padded through the mud to the Borough's gate. Setting his eye to the peep-hole, his nose pressed against the wood, he peered through. A lantern hanging on the gate's other side made a small pool of yellow light; beyond that was intense darkness.

'Who are you?' the door-keeper barked. 'Speak up and don't keep me standing here in the cold all night.'

The shadows moved. The black shape of a man moved nearer to the light, but not into it. A weary voice said, 'I am Kenelm. Of the North Saxons.'

'Oh. Kenelm of the North Saxons, are you? Whatever are you a-doing here, my lord, honouring us unworthy ones with your presence?'

'I'm tired. I'm hungry, I'm wet and I'm cold. Let me in.'

'These gates close at sunset,' said the door-keeper, 'and they don't open again until sunrise, not for anybody. I'm sure it's the same in the land of the North Saxons. Go to the guest house. You'll find fuel set for a fire, and blankets and food. Come back after sunrise.'

The man outside half turned away, but then sharply turned back. He moved closer, into the edge of the light, speaking as he did so. The light shone on teeth above and below, on bright eyes and shaggy hair and blood and, startled, the door-keeper snatched back his head, his heart jumping for a beat or two, and whatever was said, he didn't hear.

Nerving himself, the door-keeper set his eye to the peep-hole again. He saw a tall man with a wolf-skin draped around him. The wolf's mask was on his head, with bared teeth, and its shaggy pelt mingled with his long hair and beard. There were dark stains on the wolf-fur and on the man's clothing, and his face was so thin and drawn as to be gaunt. It put the door-keeper in mind of the berserkers in stories: wild men who drank blood and fought frenziedly in battle and wore the skins of bears and wolves. The door-keeper was glad of the thick wooden gate between him and the visitor.

'What did you say?' the door-keeper shouted.

'I said, I am come with messages. News. Of the North Saxons. I wish to speak with your thane.'

He was soft-spoken, this wolf-man, not frenzied at all. Taking courage, the door-keeper shouted, 'Wish in one hand and shit in the other and see which gets full the quickest. Now off with you to the guest-house and don't come back until morning.' With satisfaction, the door-porter slammed shut his peep-hole, and went back to his fire.

It was early morning, and cold. Damp hung in the air and the light was so faint and fragile it barely disturbed the darkness. Only the first birds had begun to cheep. Through the Borough's gate and across the wooden bridge that crossed its surrounding ditch came the field workers, straggling along in twos and threes, shivering in their thin clothes.

On the other side of the ditch, beside the cart-track, stood the guest-house, a small, thatched, timber building. From its door emerged a solitary figure, moving slowly, as if his joints and muscles were stiff. He made towards the Borough's gate.

As he came closer, the field-workers stared. They drew together and whispered, indicating him with their eyes or with the tiniest of nods, afraid to point openly. The stranger was tall, but bony, his hair and beard untidy. He wore a wolf's skin, its limp, clawed paws dangling at his chest. As he passed them, they saw the wolf's thick tail hanging behind him, its tip dragging on the ground. No one dared to laugh.

The guards on the gatehouse stared too. As the stranger came into the light of the lanterns, they saw that his torn and crumpled clothes had once been coloured. They saw the wolf's fur matted with black stains, and smelt the stink of wolf and of old blood. But they made no attempt to stop the man. It was sunrise, and the gates were open for all to come and go.

The stranger passed through the gatehouse, with its brilliant lantern light and scent of timbers, and left by the further door. He came out into the damp and greyness of the early morning again, but now he was inside the Borough's high earth banks.

A walkway of logs led away from the guardhouse between patches of cultivated ground, and pens holding goats or pigs. Houses were dotted here and there among the holdings: flimsy, leaning things, built of small timbers woven together and daubed with a mixture of mud, straw and dung. Women fed chickens or tended smoky fires burning outside the doors, while children tottered nearby. They saw the stranger in the wolf-skin, and stopped in their work or play to watch him. Some of the bolder children followed him, pretending to be hounds on a wolf's trail, and some of the women came too, curious to find out who the stranger was, and why he had come.

Further on the houses were more substantial, built of planking and set in fenced yards. Many had wells within the fences, and almost all had small kitchen-huts built in the yards. Some were shops as well as houses, with large windows facing the street whose shutters were now being thrown open and goods for sale set out or hung up. But even here there were people who, on seeing the stranger in the wolf-skin and his followers, shut up shop again, or escaped from their chores, and followed. Once the stranger stopped and turned. The two children who were catching at the wolf's dangling tail fled back to the little crowd who had halted at a distance. The stranger and the crowd looked coolly at each other for a moment, then the stranger turned and went on, and the crowd followed.

At the Borough's centre was the thane's hall, a swept, paved yard before it. The guards at the hall's door straightened at the sight of the crowd coming towards them, led by a gaunt, dirty man wearing a wolf's skin.

The stranger walked straight towards the guards, his head up, and demanded, 'Who is thane here?'

The guards looked at the wolf's mask on his head, at the fur matted with dried blood and the dangling paws. They looked at the tangled hair and beard. One of them said, 'Aelfric, mate.'

'I need to speak with him,' the stranger said.

The guards studied him measuringly. His clothes, though crumpled, stained, dirty and torn, had been coloured and decorated with embroidery; and there were boots on his feet. Not a poor man then. But nevertheless travelling on foot and alone.

The other guard said, 'You'll get your chance when he holds court. Go round to the kitchens, I should. They'll give you something to eat and it's warm. Keep out their way though, if you know what's good for you.'

The stranger sighed, and pulled at the wolf's legs, which were loosely knotted across his throat. When they were untied, the guards saw the torc he wore, of twisted gold and silver wires. The finials, resting on his collar-bones, were of gold, inlaid with blue and red enamel. Both guards straightened. Not only was the man not poor, he was rich. And possibly even noble.

'If you'll wait a moment, er – lord – I'll fetch somebody.'

And that somebody fetched somebody else; a whole string of servants fetched in rapid succession, each one of higher standing than the one before – and then the stranger was led to a guest lodging, with the curious crowd following and growing larger all the time.

In the lodging he was brought hot water to wash in, and asked if he would like to lie down on the bed while food and fresh clothes were brought to him. 'Thane Aelfric cannot see you before after-noon at the earliest, my lord. But he will be told that you're here. I know he will want to welcome you to the night-meal.'

Thane Aelfric came himself to the lodgings to see his guest. The stranger was now washed and combed, and dressed in clean clothes, but the blood-stained wolf-skin was thrown over the bed, filling the room with a stink of wolf.

Aelfric seated himself on the lid of a carved chest and said, 'You gave your name to my people as "Kenelm of the North Saxons".'

'I am Kenelm Atheling. My uncle was King Guthlac.'

'Was?'

'I've come to bring you the news.'

Aelfric squinted as he carefully studied the face of the man opposite him. 'I saw King Guthlac once, a few years ago. I'd know him if I saw him again. I think. I don't know you.'

'I wasn't his heir. He had many nephews, and I was – am – one of the youngest and least important.'

'So any man could claim,' Aelfric said. 'You come here on foot and alone – why should I believe you?'

'Why should you?' Kenelm said. 'Let me tell my story, and then choose whether to believe me or not.'

'Come to the night-meal then,' Aelfric said, rising. 'I'll feed you, at least. You can tell your story before everyone, and we'll all listen.'

The thane's hall was large enough, and well-built, but not splendid, as King Guthlac's hall had been. The roof was of shingle, but not gilded. The leaning posts which buttressed the outer walls were not carved; and there was only a very little carving on the door.

Inside, the walls were hung with hangings, but plain ones, without patterning or pictures. The long tables were set out, and the thane's personal company of men were seated at those nearest the middle of the hall, where the most light and heat from the fire was concentrated.

Kenelm sat beside Aelfric, at his table at the centre of the hall. No women were present, it not being a special occasion. And, it not being a special occasion, the food was plain: pork seethed with leeks and other herbs, served on a thick trencher of stale bread. Kenelm had little to say for himself while he ate, and only half-listened to Aelfric talking about his pigs, and the quarrels among his villagers.

'But you have a story to tell,' Aelfric said, in a louder voice, when he saw that Kenelm had not only eaten the food before him, but half of the gravy-soaked trencher too. People at the nearer tables quietened. They were going to hear a new story.

Kenelm laid down his knife and looked up at his audience. They were watching him, waiting.

He said, 'All my life I've been known as Kenelm. Kenelm Atheling. Kenelm Wodensson. But I'm tired of being Kenelm. I don't want to be him any more.

Still, I'll tell you what happened to Kenelm, and to the North Saxons . . .

'A plague came . . .

2

An errand

Let me tell you about the time Kenelm was in the
monastery, a life so dreary that a bout of illness
would have come as a relief. The brothers and sisters
first rose at midnight. In the darkness, guided by
faint lantern-light, they walked from their
dormitories through wet grass that soaked their feet
and the hems of their robes, to the cold, dark church
where, trying not to yawn, they shuffled into their
places. The church was small, its windows tall and
narrow and, even at noon it was dark inside. At night,
with few candles lit, the corners and the high,
raftered roof were full of dense shadows. On the

wall behind the altar were paintings, but the gloom dulled the colours to brown. As they prayed, standing throughout, the candle-clock burned down – slowly – through three divisions. Three long hours.

They returned to bed until it was light – which, in summer, might be almost as soon as they had lain down again. Another hour, or two, was spent praying in the church, before they breakfasted on bread, butter and ale. They ate in their hall, with its plain, lime-washed walls, standing at tables of pale, scrubbed oak. There were no decorations anywhere, and the brothers all wore robes of undyed wool, in its natural colours of black or grey.

The sisters stood at tables on the other side of the hall, and they too dressed in long, straight robes of black or grey. The only way it could be told that they were women was that their heads were completely covered in close-fitting hoods, hiding their hair, showing only their faces. Kenelm often peered at them from under his brows – he might be punished for staring openly – but they hardly looked like the same creatures he remembered from his life at court.

True, he hadn't been much interested in women then – still, he could remember their long, thick plaits, their girdled waists and brightly coloured dresses; their necklaces and brooches of gold, amber and garnets. He often spent a long time thinking about them.

No one spoke during the meal except for the brother or sister appointed to read aloud from an account of a saint's life. When they had eaten, the Lady Abbess, or her deputy the Abbot, would announce the penances to be done by any member of the house who had disobeyed – this one would fast for a day, that one would do extra work, or go without sleep. Following that, the day's duties would be given out: who was to work in the kitchens, who on the farm.

But before work began, they returned to the church to stand through the service called 'High Mass'. Kenelm looked forward to this because a little more light seeped into the small church. The altar-furnishing gleamed in stray beams of light, and gold-threads and richly coloured embroidery silks made the altar-cloth beautiful. Above, on the wall, the colours in the painting of Christ in Majesty glowed. After the grey of dawn, the white walls, the grey robes, it was such relief to the eye to see the colours.

Dinner followed, a plain stew of bacon, onions and beans, eaten with a great lump of black bread and washed down with ale. As before, the meal was eaten standing and in silence, except for the thin voice of the reader. Kenelm was hungry, ate all he was given and still wanted more, but while he ate he remembered the feasts at court, where the long hall would be lit with many, many candles and torches, where the walls would be hung with brilliantly coloured hangings, and where the guests sat on benches, wearing bright clothing ornamented with gold and jewels. Colour everywhere you looked. The married women would have their hair covered with linen, but the hair of the unmarried girls would be spread over their shoulders, or woven into plaits with coloured ribbons.

The bread at court would have been made from the finest flour, so it was pale brown, almost white. There would have been fish, and roast meat – perhaps a bird, perhaps venison or pork. If there had been a stew, it would have had a thick sauce, flavoured with herbs and fruit. To drink, there would have been wine.

Instead of a reader, reading about the depressing goodness of a saint, there would have been harpists, singers, storytellers – telling of battles and monsters and lovers. Stories worth hearing. And, after the feast, lovers would have gone to their beds together. Kenelm peered again at the thin, grey-robed nuns on the other side of the room.

After dinner came the work of the day, and Kenelm was glad to go to it. He was happy to do the heaviest physical work there was to be done – at that time, in the spring, he was digging the monastery's vegetable gardens, where he would later plant beans, onions, turnips and carrots. It was a cold day, but the sun shone bright over the turned earth. Kenelm grew hot as he stabbed and heaved with the spade, but then a chill breeze would cool him. Robins and starlings lighted down to investigate the patch he had dug, and then jumped into the air again. It was not the worst of days.

Needing a break from digging, he went to the muck-heap and filled a barrow with muck from the byres and stables. The heap steamed in the cold air as he broke into it, and released a rich, pungent stink. He wheeled the heavy load back to the garden, revelling in the effort it took to move it and the proof of his own strength. It was lowly work for a son of Woden, an atheling of a royal house, but at least it was work that made him strong and kept him strong. Sitting indoors copying black marks to make books wouldn't do that. If he had still been living the life he had been born for, he would be a warrior by now, trained to fight with sword, shield and spear while wearing a helmet and a heavy chainmail coat.

He would be feasting in the King's hall. He would have a wife, and every night he would unpin her linen headdress and let down her long, thick fair hair . . .

Instead he was here, shovelling shit and praying, half-starved, and never getting nearer to a woman than peeking at the nuns across the width of the dining hall.

When work was done, in the early evening, everyone would be called to church again, to recite more prayers among the pools of candlelight and shadows, and the scent of wood released from the church's wooden pillars and walls.

The supper following the service would be another meal of bread and ale, but as a reward for a day's obedience, the monks were allowed to speak to their brothers, and the nuns to their sisters. Nuns never spoke to monks, nor monks to nuns, except when the Lady Abbess had some reason for speaking to a monk or to the Abbot, and those meetings were brief. Kenelm's neighbours found something to say, making chit-chat about how hot it had been in the kitchen, or how the Abbot had been in a bad temper, but Kenelm would sit thinking about what far more interesting subjects the world outside the monastery had to discuss. Wars, raids, scandals . . . Even the doings of pigs would be interesting if they weren't the same old monastery pigs.

The day – every day – ended with more prayers in the church, and then they went to bed. In the summer it would still be broad daylight. At midnight they rose again, to pray.

This was to be his life. No one had asked him whether he wished to be a monk. At the age of seven he had been sent from his own home to be raised at the court of his uncle, King Guthlac. But that he had expected, and he wanted to be a thane and a warrior, like his father, like his uncles. He had promised himself that he would be the strongest, the bravest . . . At ten years old he had been growing tall and strong, and learning to use weapons well. It seemed entirely possible to him that he would be the strongest and bravest fighting man of the North Saxons. That was when his uncle had given him to the Christian church, to be made a monk.

Cheated. He had been cheated. He stabbed his spade into the soil three times, each time with greater strength and vehemence. Then he leant on it, breathing hard. He had been given no choice, and he had no choice. The King was not only his lord, but his uncle, and he was bound to obey him by blood and duty. If he had been merely one of the

17

King's men, he would have gone into battle at the King's order, would have taken wounds, even died, without question. Anything less would have dishonoured him.

Well, the King had ordered him to be a Christian monk. It made no sense. King Guthlac was no Christian. He believed devoutly that he was descended from the warrior's God, Woden, and gave the other gods – Thunor, Ing, Eostre, Freya – their due worship too. But if King Guthlac wished his nephew, Kenelm, to be a Christian monk, he didn't have to explain himself.

I hate my life, Kenelm thought. It isn't fair.

Life wasn't fair.

But to have to spend his life like this, like a field-worker, digging and carting muck, going to bed with the birds and rising in the dark . . .

He thought again about running away, as he had many times before – but where could he go? How would he live? No man of wealth or reputation would take him into his war-band without knowing his name and family – which he could not give without shaming his family – and anyway, he had never completed his training, so he could never become a warrior. He would have to train among boys much younger, and he would be laughed at.

He was trapped in the monastery, trapped in this miserable life. He would grow old and die here, without ever having a chance to do any of the things that a man – and a son of Woden, an atheling – should do.

The Christians taught that whatever hardships came your way in life, you should thank God for them, and endure them patiently, for He tested hardest those He loved the most. The Christians, in their preaching, tried hard to make this seem brave and noble, but to Kenelm it was a slavish, craven fawning.

Privately, in his own head, Kenelm had stayed stubbornly loyal to his own Gods through all his years in the monastery. He had never stopped praying to Them, and most often he prayed to his ancestor, Woden. He prayed now, as he dug and shovelled muck. Show me a way out of this place. Open up a door for me. Help me to see a way I can return to my true life without disgracing my family, and everything I do, I'll do for You.

From the other side of the wooden palisade surrounding the monastery came the thump and rattle of horse's hoofs, the jangle of harness and then the shout of a man's voice. Kenelm paused in his work to listen. The breeze blew cold on him, chilling his sweat. Horses. '*The joy of thanes*,' said the poem. '*A horse gives freedom to seek adventure and visit far-off places*.' It gave Kenelm a pain, a real pain in his chest, to think that once there had been horses for him to ride, and now there were not.

The horse's hoofs turned in at the monastery's gate and entered the yard. A man shouted again, his voice carrying in the cold air.

Travellers, Kenelm thought, who had decided for some reason to break their journey here. Maybe they were Christians themselves. Where had they come from, he wondered, and where were they going? He wanted to drop his spade, find them, and ask them these questions, but he went on digging, knowing that he would only be punished if he left his work. For the punishment itself he hardly cared, but it was so galling for him, an atheling, a son of Woden, to have to bow his head, and keep silent, and meekly submit to missing his evening meal or emptying the cess-pits because he had committed some crime such as looking openly at a nun. It was less annoying to keep the rules and avoid the penances.

He worked on, bending and levering at the heavy soil, the muscles of his back and hips and arms twanging, his sweat running. His mind slipped from thoughts of the travellers to thoughts of the only journeys he had ever made – the first one, from his home to the court, and his last one, from the court to this place. He began remembering his home, his mother, his younger brothers – what they looked like had quite gone from him. He remembered the court again: the business, the crowds, the music, the colours . . . So absorbed was he by work and memory that he forgot the arrival of the travellers. When a red-faced monk from the kitchens came hurrying over to him, calling his name, he was startled, and jumped.

'Kenelm! Brother Abbot wants to see you. Right away! He's in the dining-hall.'

Kenelm straightened, feeling his back ache. He thought: *What have I done? I haven't overslept, I haven't been greedy at table, I haven't been sulky or unwilling – at least I don't think I have. Maybe someone else thinks I have. Or – has someone seen me looking at the nuns*? To the monk, he said, 'What does he want?'

'I don't know. I have to get back. Go straight away!' Turning, the monk made off, at a run, to the kitchens.

Kenelm thrust his spade into the earth and ran himself, towards the dining hall. It never occurred to him that Woden was answering his prayers.

3

The mission

The monastery was neither large nor rich, and the dining-hall where the brothers and sisters ate was often used for other business. Kenelm arrived hot and panting at its door, and almost careered on into the hall itself, but remembered himself in time. He stopped, drawing in great, rough breaths, and wiped his wet face on his sleeve. Then he pulled his robe straight, folded his hands in front of him, and walked demurely inside.

In the middle of the hall, in the space between the tables, stood three men, eating bread and drinking from the monastery's earthenware cups. They wore helmets, and coats of mail, and swords slung from their shoulders. A thrill went through Kenelm as he recognised them as house-carls, the kept warriors of some rich thane. Quickly looking round, peering beneath his brows without lifting his head, he spotted their shields and spears leaning against the wall. The shields were painted red, with a white dragon at their centres. Kenelm's heart jumped and began to thump briskly. The white dragon on a red ground was his uncle's badge. These were King Guthlac's men.

Father Abbot was standing a little apart from the house-carls and, hurrying over to him, Kenelm bowed. As always, he had to grit his teeth against his own anger. The Abbot, before he had become a Christian, had been a nothing, a no one – a freeman, it was true, but a grubber in the earth, a churl, a swine-herd. And Kenelm, an atheling and a Son of Woden, had to bow to him. 'All men and women are brothers and sisters in Christ,' the Abbot often said. 'Within these walls there are no thanes and no churls.' Like so much the Christians said, it was a lie. The Abbot was a thane here, but he was a swine-herd set up as a thane, and the thanes were made churls and had to bow to him. Kenelm never found it easy.

'Father Abbot, I was told you wanted to see me.'

'Where have you been?' said the Abbot. 'How long does it take you to come from the garden?' Kenelm set his teeth and didn't answer. 'There is water and a towel,' the Abbot said, pointing to one of the long trestle tables at which the monks ate. On its corner was set a large earthenware bowl and a folded towel. 'Wash your hands and face – quickly! The Lady Abbess wishes to see you.'

As ever, the Abbot's face softened, and his voice became reverential when he mentioned the Abbess. Kenelm would have been amused if he hadn't been so astonished. He couldn't remember the last time the Lady Abbess had spoken to a mere monk, and he couldn't imagine why she wished to speak to him. What had he done? And why were the house-carls here? Anywhere else he could simply have asked, but in the monastery such curiosity would be called a sin, like so many other things, and would earn him a penance.

'Don't stand there!' the Abbot said. 'Be quick! The Lady is waiting.'

Kenelm went hurriedly to the table and washed his dirty hands and sweaty face in the cool, brown water the bowl held. Hastily he dried himself on the rough towel, and then again presented himself to the Abbot who, without a word, led the way from the hall. Kenelm looked over his shoulder as he went, and saw that the house-carls remained behind.

The Abbot, in silence, led the way through the monastery yards, past the church, to the long dormitory where the nuns slept. At one end of this building were the Abbess' private quarters, just as the Abbot's private quarters were attached to the monk's dormitory.

Monks weren't allowed to enter the nun's dormitory, but the Abbess' room could be reached by a flight of outer stairs – little more than a stout ladder – which led from the mud of the yard to the building's upper storey. The Abbot climbed first. Kenelm waited patiently, amusing himself by watching the Abbot's bare, bony, ugly ankles, and the hairy legs above them. When the Abbot was almost at the top of the ladder, Kenelm carefully made his face blank, and followed.

The Abbess' room was small and dimly lit even though it was daylight outside. Light entered only by the door and by one small window. A sweet smell of wood came from the walls, and of lavender and old grass from the straw and herbs strewn on the floor.

In one corner, tidily rolled, was the straw-filled mattress which the Abbess unrolled at night and spread on the floorboards for her bed. Hanging on the back wall was a large, plain wooden crucifix and, beneath it, a big wooden chest for storing parchments. Under the window, where the light was best, the Abbess sat on her stool at her table, with parchments, quill, knife and ink-horn before her. There was no other furniture.

'Lady.' Standing before the table, the Abbot bowed his head. Kenelm, though nervous, had time to notice that the back of the Abbot's neck had flushed, and his voice had become gentle. 'Here is Brother Kenelm.'

The Abbess set down her quill, sat straight on her stool and looked beyond the Abbot to Kenelm. She was not a young woman, but her age was difficult to guess. It was her habit to eat less than any of her nuns, and the skin of her face stretched so tightly over her bones that it scarcely had room to wrinkle. The bony edges of her eye-sockets were plainly visible. For the rest, she was almost colourless. Since she spent little time in the open air, her skin was smooth and white as milk. Her eyes were such a pale blue, they were only a shade or two darker than the whites, and her lashes could hardly be seen. Her lips were so pale, they were almost the same colour as the rest of her face. All her hair was hidden away under a close-fitting white cap, and the robe that covered her thin body from the neck down was grey. Kenelm thought her ugly – wilfully, deliberately ugly – and again, longingly, he remembered the women of the court, with their rich colouring and bright clothes.

'Thank you, Brother Abbot,' she said, 'for bringing the brother to me.' Her voice was soft and quiet, with a foreign accent, since she came from a country to the South, where the people were mostly Christian and monasteries were common. When talk was allowed at table in the evening, the monks sometimes said that, in her own country, the Abbess had been a princess. Certainly she was an educated woman, who could read and write.

So in love with Christ was she, went the story, that He was the only husband she would accept, and she had become a nun. The monks seemed thrilled by the thought of their house being led by a princess. Kenelm couldn't understand why a princess – a daughter of Woden – would choose to deny Him and become the celibate 'bride' of a celibate husband.

'Brother Kenelm,' she said, calling him to attention, 'I have bad news for you, may God save us. The King has sent word, asking if you might return to the Royal Borough.'

Bad news? Kenelm thought. It was the best possible news. His uncle had sent for him! He was to return to the court – that wonderful place of bustle and colour and life!

A realisation burst on him. This was the answer to his prayers! He had asked, and Woden had granted. He felt himself filled with sunshine and lightness, and for an instant felt that he might float off the ground, brilliance shining from his eyes and ears. He was quite dizzy with awe and thankfulness.

'You were a gift to the church, were you not?' the Abbess said. When he didn't answer, she stared at him with her colourless eyes from inside the rim of her white headdress. 'Were you not?'

Kenelm, starting from his delight, coughed. 'Yes, Lady.'

She lifted a corner of a parchment and studied it. 'I would not normally grant permission –'

Kenelm's heart sank heavily, like a stone into deep water.

'– but there are special circumstances. Therefore I grant you a month's leave.'

Kenelm's spirits rose again, swinging giddily high. The Abbess said something but, deafened by anticipation of the court, he didn't hear it. The Abbot's hard, bony fingers prodded him in the back.

'Receive her blessing,' the Abbot hissed.

Kenelm went forward and, beside the table, dropped to his knees with a thump on the wooden floor. A smell of lavender rose from the crushed herbs. All he could see was the skirt of the Abbess' grey gown, as it fell from her sharp knee-bones to the wooden floor. It started him thinking of rounder knees and fuller, more curved thighs—

'While you are away from the protection of this house,' said the Abbess' voice, dragging him from his thoughts, 'you are not to forget yourself. You are to pray every morning, every noon and every evening. Do you promise me that?'

'I promise you I will pray, Lady,' said Kenelm. He thought: I shall pray to Woden.

'Your leave is for a month only. At the end of that time, you will return here, to be shriven and cleansed of the outside world, and made fit to be among us again. You understand?'

'I understand, Lady,' Kenelm said. He was glad she did not make him promise, in exact words, to return.

He felt her hand, small and light, touch his head. 'May God have you in His keeping while you are away from us,' she said. 'May He smile on all you do and say.'

Her hand was withdrawn, and Kenelm stood.

'You will leave early tomorrow morning,' the Abbess said. 'With the escort the King has sent. Before then you will make your confession and spend the evening in prayer – in a state of Grace, you will be better prepared to resist the world outside.' She contemplated him with a long look. 'Until you return, my prayer shall be that God will keep you safe.'

Return? Kenelm thought. Now Woden has opened the gates for me, I shall never be so ungrateful as to return through them.

'I shall hear Brother Kenelm's confession myself,' the Abbot said.

The Abbess nodded. 'Thank you, Father.'

The Abbot bridled like a complimented girl. 'Come along, Brother. The Abbess is busy. We must not disturb her further.'

They both bowed to the Abbess, and Kenelm followed the Abbot down the ladder into the yard. Confession was an unpleasant chore, especially to the Abbot, who would impose endless prayers . . . But then, it would make a welcome change to spend the rest of the day in prayer. If he prostrated himself on the church floor, he could even take the weight off his feet. And he would be sure to find his way back to the dining-hall for the evening meal. He wasn't going to miss that.

Kenelm had not ridden a horse since he'd been given to the monastery, and he had to keep correcting his balance and thinking about how the reins should fit in his fingers. The horse's bones and his bones jolted together uncomfortably, but he would have endured far more pain before dismounting. This was how an atheling was meant to travel, on horseback, and he would not give it up.

The house-carls rode easily. Their leader stayed close beside Kenelm, occasionally putting out a hand to help with Kenelm's horse if it became too frisky. 'Hadn't you heard of the Sickness?' he said.

Kenelm shrugged. Perhaps the Lady Abbess had heard. Perhaps the Abbot had. But they would have kept it to themselves. 'I don't hear news,' he said.

'Everybody's sick and in bed,' said the house-carl. 'Nearly everybody. That's why there's only the three of us for your escort. We'm the only three fit enough to ride.'

'Never mind,' said one of the other men. 'The bandits won't bother us. They're all in bed shivering and puking.'

The third man had a white, bald scar running through his beard on one cheek. He said, 'I'm only just over it meself. Bad business. Me head ached all day. Ached when I got up. Ached when I went to bed. Never stopped. Felt like me head was crammed full of big rocks, and I couldn't hardly hold it up. Throbbing and banging. If somebody had come and chopped it off, I'd have thanked 'em.'

'Sore throat I had,' said the second man.

'Aye,' said the third. 'Every time I breathed, it was like somebody was polishing me weasand with scouring sand. It was like a giant had got hold of the back of me neck and was squeezing hard. Me knees and me shoulders and me elbows and every little joint of me toes and fingers all ached together. Misery! There was no way I could sit or lie or stand that give me any comfort.' He paused to wipe his nose on his fingers, and flicked the snot away into the bushes that bordered the path, before wiping his fingers on his breeches. 'And then, next day, shaking started! I got hotter and hotter, as if I was in the bath-house. Me head felt like it was swelling and was going to go POP! And I was shaking with heat! Not cold, with heat! Me bones was jangling, me teeth was dancing, and still me joints ached and me head and me throat was sore. Oh, it was bad, I'm telling you. I still don't feel well in meself.'

The leader of the men said, 'That's why there's nobody about.'

They were following a path through the forest, a place of open, grassy glades, and tall trees, still bare of leaves, though here and there a green haze showed about the grey branches. For some time Kenelm had felt there was something odd about the scene, something wrong – but it had been so long since he'd left the monastery, he didn't trust his instinct. Now he realised that the forest was deserted.

He remembered his childhood, when he had wandered in the forest. It had always been a busy place. A hunt, of course, with all its horses and riders, and dogs, and beaters and kennel-men and attending servants, made a great to-do. But a forest was also thronged with swine-herds and their swine, cattle-herds and their cattle, goose-herds and their geese; by woodsmen tending the coppices and spinneys, by women and children searching for firewood, or mushrooms, or nuts or berries, depending on the time of year. There were reeves, officers of the thane or lord, making sure that no one was grazing more animals than they were allowed, or taking more wood. And then there were the people making their way, on foot, or on horse, mule, cart or donkey, to other hamlets, or to outlying fields.

Now the wide spaces between the trees were

empty, except for deer. They passed geese and swine wandering untended.

'The King's in bed,' said the house-carls' leader. 'The Queen's in bed.'

'I was in bed meself,' said Scar-Beard. 'For a good week. Snot was pouring from me nose like water from a jug. Me lips was all hot and split, and I'd wiped me nose so often it was sore as a carbuncle. I was so thirsty I could have drunk the seas dry but I'd no appetite at all. I couldn't sit up without me head thumping, let alone stand. A two-year-old babby girl could have thrashed me with one hand.'

They neared the Royal Borough, and the fields that surrounded it were empty. Cows, sheep and pigs wandered on the common land without anyone to watch them.

'I still don't know,' Kenelm said, 'why the King has sent for me.'

'Not the King,' said the captain. 'The King's sick. It was Aelderman Egwin who sent for you, in the King's name.'

'But why?'

'He'll explain it better than me,' said the captain.

The Royal Borough came in sight. A high bank of earth, limed white and shining in the sun, was topped by a timber stockade, also limed. A narrow bridge led across the deep ditch to the white-painted timber gatehouse. Flags fluttered from the gatehouse's roof. As they unfolded in the wind, they showed a white dragon on a red ground. The Borough gave Kenelm a shock – after the dull monastery it was so big, so fine – and it brought so much back to him: the noise of hunts and the music of feasts, the colour, the business, the *life*.

There was one guard on the gate, and he didn't look well. He leaned heavily on his spear and hardly glanced up as the small party rode through the gate and into a silent, empty Royal Borough.

They clopped along a muddy track beside a timber walkway, passing small huts where no smoke rose from the roofs. There were no people to be seen in the yards or garden plots, except one small child playing in the mud. A pig and a flock of hens were wandering loose.

A second ditch and bank enclosed the King's hall itself. There were two guards on the gatehouse here, but one was coughing hard. Once they were through the gate, Scar-Beard reined in. 'I'll stable the hosses,' he said. 'Somebody's got to see to the poor beasts.'

They dismounted, and Scar-Beard led the horses away. The other two men led Kenelm through empty yards, past the great Royal Feast Hall, past the God-

House with its carved dragons, past the Queen's Bower, and the lesser halls of many nobles, to the hall where Aelderman Egwin lived.

The hall was not a large one, though it was fine in its own modest way. The roof was shingled, and the door beautifully carved with dragons, painted red and green. The paved area around it, though, was muddy and unswept, strewn with dirty straw and old leaves. Kenelm was nervous as they approached the door and, without knowing it, clenched his back teeth together and balled his hands tightly into fists. Why had he been sent for? What if it wasn't to set him free from the monastery, but to punish him for something? For what? He'd been in the monastery for years, without the chance to do anything wrong. Not anything that King Guthlac would consider wrong anyway.

The doors of the hall stood slightly ajar, and the house-carls pushed them wide and led the way in. Inside, the long building was dim and full of shadows, lit only by a fire burning towards the upper end. There was a smell of smoke and burning, and less pleasant smells too: sewer smells of stale piss, and dung; nasty whiffs of vomit and sweaty bodies. Strange sounds too: grating, wheezing sounds, snuffling and grunting. The dimness made it hard to see, after coming in from the daylight outside, but then Kenelm glimpsed the people lying on the floor of the hall. All across the width of the hall and down its length, people were lying on the floor, huddled in blankets, shaking and sneezing and coughing.

Kenelm and his companions picked their way through the sick, making their way towards the upper end of the hall, where the private rooms were. Kenelm covered his mouth and nose with his hands, hoping not to breathe in the sickness.

A young woman hurried towards them through the sprawled sick. She looked both worried and scared – a kitchen maid perhaps, who would not have greeted guests in the normal way of things.

'I'm sorry, my lords – you see how it is – can I help you?'

One of the house-carls said, 'This is Kenelm Atheling. Lord Egwin is expecting him. I know the way.'

The girl gawped at Kenelm and cringed into a sort of curtsy. They passed her by, making their way through and over the sick to the end of the hall, where the captain drew aside a curtain and knocked loudly on the door behind it.

A voice from inside, muffled by the wooden walls and woollen hangings, shouted, 'Come in!' The captain opened the door and stood aside for Kenelm to enter alone.

The room behind the door was lit by a single thick candle standing on a chest but, being a small space, was more brightly illuminated than the hall. Besides the chest the only other furnishings were the saffron-coloured hangings on the walls, and a great wooden-framed bed. In the bed, propped up on cushions, was a big old man, with long faded hair and a long beard, wiping his nose and eyes on a piece of rag. He looked up, his blue eyes angry.

Kenelm shut the door behind him. 'Good day, your lordship. I'm sorry to see you ill. How do you feel?'

'Much as always,' said the old man, his voice hoarse. 'My joints ache every day – an ache more here or there, a sore throat, a pain in the head, is nothing to me. Not like you youngsters, who think every little twinge means your death. Sit down – ah . . .' After a brief struggle with his memory, he finished the sentence: 'Sit down, boy.' Kenelm sat on the edge of the bed. The old man peered at him. 'Thank you for coming,' he said, as if Kenelm had been free to refuse. 'How are things at the – what do they call it? – that place where you live?'

'The monastery, my lord? All is as usual,' Kenelm said guardedly.

'The sickness isn't there yet?'

'No, my lord. Everyone is well. I hadn't even heard of the sickness.'

'So you're still well yourself?'

'Perfectly well, my lord,' Kenelm said.

'Good, good. As I hoped. I think you're the only member of the Royal Kin still on his feet. Tell me, boy, are you a Christian?'

The question took Kenelm by surprise and he didn't know how to answer. He supposed that since his uncle had given him to the monastery, he had wanted him to become a Christian. 'I was sent to the monastery, my lord, when I was ten.'

'No, no, no,' the old man said. 'I mean are you truly a Christian? I daresay you've learned all the right things to say, but do you believe any of it? Does it matter to you?'

Kenelm wondered what answer the old man wanted to hear. 'Ah. Well.'

'Oh, come along, come along.' The old man wiped his nose again. 'I don't give a fart which god or goddess you worship – or even if you worship none at all. But I need to know: Are you a Christian?'

'Well, my lord,' Kenelm said carefully, 'it was my uncle the King who ordered that I should be taught—'

'On my advice. If we are to have Christians in the

40

kingdom, setting up their colleges and converting our people, then we should have our people among them. That's what I told your uncle, and he agreed.'

So it's you I have to thank for the last few years, Kenelm thought. You old wretch. Why did you have to pick me? He said, 'If you want the truth, the more they teach me about Christ, the less I believe any of it. Christ is the only god, they say, but as far as I can tell, he's just Ing called by another name. They say theirs is the "Lord of Peace" but isn't that exactly what we say—'

'Yes, yes,' the old man broke in. 'I don't want to listen to any of that.' His voice sounded as if it would choke to a stop at any moment. 'I only asked because I need you to run an errand, and it was important to know if this Christ business would be a hindrance to you. But I take it that it won't be. Good.'

An errand? Kenelm's mind quickened, turning over many possibilities.

'I've been brought some bad news,' Egwin said. 'A Foreign raiding party – maybe more than one – is on its way. They've heard of the sickness, you can be sure, and are out to make the best of it.'

Kenelm stood and, distracted, walked to the door, turned and came back again. 'But – what do you want me to do? It's been – it's been *years* since I had a sword and shield in my hands.' Look what's become of your clever plan, he thought. What was the use of knowing that God was One and Three, or of being able to spell His name, when raiders were coming to burn houses and drive off the kingdom's wealth?

'We don't want you to fight, boy,' Egwin said. 'There are scarcely two fighting men fit to stand on their feet – are you going to fight them off all by yourself? No, what we want you to do is to deliver a message to those who *can* help – if they will.'

Kenelm was disappointed – then relieved – then disappointed again. 'Is that all?' He felt useful, important – then remembered that he was descended from Woden and a member of the Royal House. 'I'm not a messenger,' he said. Then added quickly, in case he lost the chance, 'but I'll do it.'

'Of course you will do it,' Egwin said, and coughed for a while.

Kenelm grew impatient to hear the details of his mission. 'I'm to ride to Mercia and ask for help. Ask them to send armed men.' He saw himself riding back at the head of this troop, riding back among his own people as a saviour. If he could win praise for this – if he could somehow impress the Mercians – if he could get his uncle to say, 'Well done', perhaps he would be able to leave the Christian brothers and come home to his proper life.

'Mercia is too far,' Egwin said. 'You could never bring help from there in time – even if you could talk them into giving it. No, you are to ride into the wood.'

'The wood?' A wilderness of trees and wild country. 'How will I find any help in the wood?'

'You won't find it,' Egwin said. 'It will find you.'

4

In the wood

Swine wandered loose among the trees, rooting in
the earth and gobbling fallen acorns. They trotted
briskly away with raised tails as Kenelm walked near,
his feet rustling through the layers of old leaves.
With no herder to keep them together, the swine
were roaming as they pleased.

The wide forest rides were deserted. Tawny or
bronze with depths of old leaves, the forest floor
stretched away into the distance, shadowed by green-
and-grey-barked trees. Deer picked through them,
turning their heads and cocking their ears at
Kenelm's passing.

He went on at a smart pace, despite the headache nagging behind his eyes. In imagination he saw raiders within the borders of his country, burning farms and driving off cattle, leaving behind them dead and grieving and long months of hunger. The thought kept him moving for a mile into the forest, then two. Even here, before the sickness, he might have expected to meet woodsmen, who farmed the forest, pollarding some trees, felling others – but there was no one. The forest was left to itself.

Kenelm's headache worsened and he longed to stop, but old Egwin's orders had been to pass through the forest. 'Leave the rides behind,' he'd said. 'Go deep into the wild woods, further than even the charcoal burners go.'

'How shall I know my way?' Kenelm had asked. 'Where am I going? There are no paths.'

'You don't need to find any way,' the old man had said. 'Go into the woods. Lose yourself. When you are quite lost, sit down and wait. They will find you.'

Had the old man's wits been turned by fever? 'Who will find me?'

Egwin had wiped his nose and given him a sharp, suspicious look. 'Deep in the wood, who do you think will find you?'

Kenelm's mouth opened to give the answer that

had immediately occurred to him, and stayed open as he thought better of it.

'Well?' Egwin had said.

'The . . . the Wood People?'

The Wood People who, at dusk, called the names of men and women from the shadows under the trees. If you were fooled and answered them, they led you, calling, further and further into the woods. When you grew fearful, and would not follow their calling voices any further, they came to you out of the trees, and they were so beautiful that all fear of them fell away . . . Unless, by chance, you caught a glimpse of their backs. Their backs were not of soft flesh, but like hollowed, rotten logs. Cunningly they kept their backs hidden and led their captives by the hand, still deeper into the woods, where there were wolves, wild boar and bears; further and further from home and safety. Some found their way back from the Wood People, thinking they had been lost for a single night, and found that fifty years had passed. Everything and everyone they knew had gone.

'Are you too Christian for this errand?' Egwin had asked. 'Go deep into the wood and break a twig – and They will soon come, to find the trespasser.'

The broad rides, where walking had been easy,

became more choked with scrub, with brambles and nettles. Kenelm turned aside into the bushes, ducking under branches, wading thigh-deep through high weeds and nettles, deliberately leaving behind the known, populated forest. For a while he followed a narrow footpath, where strong, juicy stems and leaves leaned over from either side, pushing against him almost as an animal might – but soon even that uncertain path vanished in the greenery, and he had to force his way through as well as he might. He called out and sang, hoping to warn any bears who might be sleeping in the thicket. It was not wise to suddenly stumble on and disturb a bear.

He won through to more open ground, where the trees discouraged growth beneath them and layered the earth with their fallen leaves, but still he had to bend and twist and weave in and out of the close-growing branches, and flounder in the depths of soft leaf-mould. He sweated with effort and, in truth, felt worse every moment. His headache was aggravated by all his ducking and turning, until he sat beneath a tree and rested his brow in his hands. He wondered if those who were to find him would soon appear and spare him the effort of going on. Perhaps they would call to him from deeper in the woods – calling his name gently, over and over, as songs and stories said the Wood People did.

Now he had stopped moving, there was no longer the sound of his feet scuffling through old leaves, nor the sound of branches being pushed aside and twigs snapping. A silence settled over the woods: a silence as thick and heavy as a winter cloak, stretching away into the distance. No birds live in the deep woods; no animals scuttle through the undergrowth. Sheltered by the trees from the wind, not even a leaf moved against another. There was no calling of his name.

In that quiet, he felt how far he was from home and help. His head throbbed. How long was he to sit there, waiting for something that might be nothing but a story – and that, if it was real, he hoped would never come? He wished for it all to be over, one way or another. Remembering old Egwin's words, he reached up to the tree above his head and bent and twisted a twig until it broke.

There was no sound, no movement. Nothing appeared before his eyes. He waited a while longer – how short or long a time he had no way of telling – and then lay down in the leaves, hoping that the aching in his head would ease.

Many thoughts and images passed through his head, mingling, confused: thoughts of the raiders, of old Egwin, of the company of Christian brothers he had left behind, of old stories . . . He didn't think that he slept, but suddenly he was startled, and rose sharply on his elbow, his heart giving a bound . . .

A woman was kneeling close by him, peering into his face. At the sight of her, his heart leaped again, swinging in his chest as if it had been struck. It was so unexpected to see her there, a woman, alone deep in the woods. And she was so beautiful, she was frightening. And she was naked.

Her eyes were dark, with brilliant whites, and the lids edged in black, pointed at their inner and outer corners. The face was narrow and sharp, and the lips thick and red, pushing forward, as if to kiss or to bite. Around her head and falling down about her were heavy masses and ropes of shining dark hair, through which pushed one naked shoulder and one bare knee. A grey spider crawled unnoticed in one tress, spinning a shining thread over the surface of the hair.

The woman spoke, and between her lips he glimpsed a sharp white tooth. She said, 'Why did you break our tree?'

Kenelm opened his mouth to speak, but he had no words ready and could only stare at her. Truth to tell, any pretty woman would have left him speechless, let alone a beautiful, naked one, and this beautiful creature was not only a woman but a Wood Woman. No mortal woman would be here, naked and alone. He knew he was in danger, but also that he had to speak. 'I was . . . I was sent to find you.'

She turned her head sidelong and looked at him from the corner of one bright, dark eye. A long skein of hair, tumbling down from her shoulder, dislodged the spider, which let itself down on a thread to the leaves below.

'Egwin Aelderman sent me,' Kenelm said. 'He told me to break your tree. He said you would find me.'

She drew back from him and smiled, her upper lip drawing back from more sharp teeth. 'Egwin?' she said, and turned from him to look behind her.

There was a faint rustle among the dead and living leaves, and a movement. Kenelm looked beyond the woman who knelt beside him and saw – something, but he was not sure what. There was something, among all the patterning of twigs and hanging leaves and trunks and branches – and then a movement, a line, a mass all seemed to snap together and he saw two other women, also naked, standing at a little distance. They came forward and stooped over him and, to his astonishment, they were exactly like the first. On these two other heads were the same heavy masses of dark hair: the same pointed faces, full red lips and clear, dark eyes. There were long, slim legs, stepping delicately like deer's legs. There were breasts, bobbing and peeping through the long dark hair. They were so beautiful that their backs had to be like hollowed, rotted logs.

'We remember Egwin,' said the first woman. 'He lives still?'

'He sent me to you with a message. And a plea.' Kenelm sat up and, as he did so, his head gave a thump, and he became aware of how stiff his neck was. It hurt as if a giant hand with a powerful grip was clenched on his nape. He tried to think of what to say next, but his mind was muzzy, and his mouth and throat dry.

The first Wood Woman leaned towards him, her mass of hair swinging forward and brushing him. The other two knelt on either side of her, looking at him intently. 'You are sick,' said the first, and her white teeth flashed between her lips. The great dark eyes of all three of them glistened.

Kenelm remembered that it is the weak rabbit, sick or young, that is taken by the fox. But he ached so much, in his head and neck, and felt so ill that he thought he might not live anyway. And he still had to deliver his message, which he had promised faithfully to deliver. The keeping of a promise, especially the promise of an atheling, a son of Woden, must come before everything. He said, 'Listen. The Foreigners are coming against us. Raiding parties. And all our men are sick. They cannot fight.'

'That is nothing to us,' said another of the women, the one furthest from him.

Kenelm felt as if he lay close by a fire. Heat was gathering inside his clothes, setting his face glowing. This was the Sickness, he realised: he was feverish. Soon he might not be able to speak. 'They'll come far into our country,' he said, his voice weak and hoarse. 'There's no one to drive them away. They'll burn farms and steal cattle. When they're gone, they'll leave famine behind.'

'This is nothing to us,' said the woman again.

The first woman turned to the others and said, 'But Egwin sends these words to us.'

'And the burning farms may burn the woods,' Kenelm said, feeling himself grow hotter yet. Little tremors were running through him. 'And the Foreigners will hunt your deer.'

The first woman, looking down at him as he sweated and trembled, said, 'Egwin wishes us to drive off these Foreigners?'

'He begs you!'

The first woman rose from her knees and stretched her arms above her head, a movement which lifted her breasts as her long hair fell back, and thrust forward her ribs. 'Egwin begs us!' she said. 'Let's hunt then! Let's track them and harry them – and sing to them in the night-time!'

The other two rose, laughing, throwing back their hair from their shoulders. 'If that's to be the game!'

'To the hunt then!'

Kenelm, lying on the ground in the leaves, started to shake. His body was hot all over, and there was a fire in his head. The hotter he was, the more he shook – and yet he looked up at the three women and for all the throbbing in his head and the fog of heat before his eyes, he thought he had never seen anything so beautiful.

The voice of the first woman rose on a long, climbing note. The voice of the second rose a moment later, intertwining with the first; and the third's voice rose too, winding in and out of the others. The voices were sharp and cool in the silence of the wood and rang out, travelling far through the trees. All three voices reached a peak together and then broke and fell, tumbling their notes around each other. Even in the heat of

Kenelm's fever, the wild song struck a chill.

Singing, the women turned, their feet trampling and rustling in the leaves, their hair flying. Stooping, one after another, they snatched up grey things, which they whirled in the air about their heads – skins. They had picked up wolf-skins. Catching the skins between both hands they stretched them over their heads, still dancing, still singing, and then lowered the skins to their shoulders. The skinned masks of wolves sat on top of their heads, baring their fangs in their dark hair. One after another the women threw themselves forward, arms outstretched, as if to land on their hands – and, bounding round him on long legs were not three women but three wolves. Shaggy and grey, brindled with tawny, they voiced their song again, before racing away through the trees, tails high, their paws kicking up dead brown leaves.

Kenelm lay down. Fever visions, he thought. He was shaking so hard that his head rattled on his neck, his arms jolted against his sides, his legs jangled and all his joints were jarred. He drew up his knees and curled into a ball, hugging himself to control the shaking. The rustling of the leaves beneath him, and the sound of his own gasping and shuddering, filled his ears. He knew that there, alone in the wood and

55

sick, he might die. But, he had done what he could. He had kept his promise, and delivered his message.

5

Wolves in the wood

Soft fronds brushed and tickled Kenelm's face. Juicy green smells rose about him as he moved. The stems and leaves he lay on creaked and rustled. He counted the time in fits of fever, when he grew hot and shook, and the welcome spells of icy coldness when the shaking stopped. A burning bear, a bear made of flames, came and talked to him, but he was so afraid it would set the trees on fire that he didn't listen to what it said, and wasn't sure it was speaking English anyway. Later, when he was cold, the bear hadn't been about, nor had it left any burned patches behind it. It had been a bear that burned without consuming, like the bush in the Bible.

He heard leaves crumpling as pads pressed them down, and the swish of a strong tail sweeping aside stems. A cold nose pressed into his neck, and he opened his sore eyes to see that the wolves had returned. The wolf nearest him lay down and rolled in the grass. Its fur parted, and a naked woman sat up from the skin like a woman rising from under a wolf-skin coverlet in the midst of a wood. 'Come and run with us,' she said.

'I can't.'

She reached out and gripped his arm hard. Tugging, she dragged him to his feet. The trees, the sky, spun around him and, dizzily looking down, he saw a man lying among the leaves and greenery. He thought it strange that another man should be there, deep in the wood, until he realised that he was looking at himself.

'Come, come,' said the woman, and pushed at his shoulder, and pulled at his hand. He started in the direction she moved him. His legs, his feet, moved, but he felt no contact with the ground. Ahead of him, through the grey and green of the wood, he saw the grey wolves loping, their tails held high. Their forelegs and ribs stretched for the stride, their paws hit the ground and kicked it behind. The third wolf quickly joined them. Kenelm tried to run faster, to stay with the wolves, and he flew – as he had in dreams – flying through the trees, above the brambles and grass and toadstool-grown logs – flying like a seed-wisp on a breeze.

Through the arches of trees – bounding across streams, plunging through thickets – mile after mile. Until the wolves stopped and threw up their heads, drawing in the air. They went on slowly, nosing through the undergrowth, slinking about trees, their heads low and their ears pricked. Kenelm hovered with them, brushing their fur, drifting with them.

A track ran through the wood, and from the track came the bawling of sheep, human laughter and singing, the sound of feet on soft, muddy earth, the trampling of hoofs. The wolves looked down through branches and twigs. Kenelm, hanging in the trees like a mist, looked down too.

Along the woodland path came a Foreign raiding party. The sheep they drove before them filled the sunken path, bobbing and surging this way and that, constantly baaaing. Men were among them, driving them with spears, shouting. The men wore coats of leather, sewn with metal rings, and had shields slung on their shoulders. Some were bareheaded, with long dark hair hanging to their shoulders; others still wore their helmets.

A wolf ran out from the trees and trotted along beside the path, lean shoulders and hips working. Just as the Foreigners glimpsed its grey shape, the wolf slipped back into the shadowed aisles of trees. On the other side of the track, another appeared. In and out, the wolves wove through the grey-green trees like grey ribbons, like skeins of smoke.

The Foreigners shouted. They pointed with spears. Turning their heads, they looked up and down the path, looking for each other. The word they cried out Kenelm did not know, but he understood it: 'Wolves! Wolves!'

Spears came flying into the forest. Arrows came. They struck trees and fell into bushes; they stuck, quivering, in the soft forest earth. And then they were lost – who would climb the steep bank from the track and duck into the wood to fetch back a spear or arrow when wolves were about?

The wolves ran ahead and crossed the track, hidden by trees and bushes, and came again on the track's other side. They yipped to make sure the men saw them, vanishing as soon as they did. Kenelm almost laughed to see the men's panic, to see them struggling to draw closer together through the sea of sheep. He knew what they were thinking – that these were strange wolves, to follow men so closely when there was no winter snow and cold to make them hungry. Strangely cunning wolves, too, to yelp and show themselves and fade away. And so large a pack – they were on either side, they were behind, they were in front. How many? Ten? Twenty?

The Foreigners made camp in the middle of the path – they were afraid of the trees – and lit a fire, not so much for warmth as for light to keep away the darkness and the wolves.

The fire flared brilliantly as dusk thickened the darkness under the trees, the red and yellow flames throwing showers of sparks into the air. The Foreigners took food from their packs, and were, for a short while, cheery. But the fire did not keep the wolves away. Quick, moving darkness flitted just outside the fire's light. Eyes flashed green. Kenelm, as he drifted through the fire's gauzy veils of light, looked down and saw the men's eyes roll, showing the whites. He heard their voices rise on a note of fear, though he couldn't understand their words.

And then, from the darkness, into the firelight, stepped three women. The men around the fire started back and got to their feet in sheer astonishment, staring. They didn't, in that first instant, feel fear.

The women's long dark hair shone in the firelight like dark water, and flowed down over their shoulders, hanging to their waists and melting into the darkness. The soft rounds of their breasts gleamed through the fall of hair. The rounds of their bellies and their long thighs caught the light. They were, between the darkness and the firelight, breathtakingly beautiful. They were terrifying.

The men huddled together, and almost backed into the darkness surrounding the fire, while the women moved to the light and the flames and knelt beside them. At the edge of the light, the men stopped, looking over their shoulders into the darkness. All day they'd been haunted by most unnatural wolves – and now these unnatural women appeared from the dark wood. They could not be mortal women.

The men drew knives from their belts and boots, or looked longingly to the spears left near the fire. But the women made no threat. They sat by the fire and spoke to each other, and laughed, and looked sideways at the men. They smoothed the heat of the fire over their skin, and smiled at the men. They combed their long hair with their fingers.

The Foreigners watched. One stooped and put his

knife back in his boot. He looked at his friends and grimaced, as if to say: Well, I'm going to take the chance. He took a couple of steps towards the fire, and paused, waiting to see what the women would do. They smiled at him and beckoned.

He went closer and, as he did, the other men took their first steps forward. The first man said something to the women. They leaned back on their arms, shaking back their hair, looked up at him and gave their widest smiles. The man sat down beside them. All the others moved at once, and sat down too.

Kenelm drifted, rising and falling in the air that rose over the fire. He watched as the women smiled at the men nearest them, and leaned against their shoulders. One twined her fingers in a man's dark, curly hair. Another kissed a man's cheek; the third touched a man's knee. The other men watched, wary but fascinated.

One man pushed away the woman who leaned on him. She smiled, shrugged, and turned to the man on her other side, who grinned at his companions and, when she kissed him, kissed her back. Another man wrapped his arms round a woman and slid one hand down her smooth back, stroked his other hand in her long hair.

And then there was snarling, and grey fur, and blood. There was outcry from frightened men and a reaching for spears and knives. The smoke swirled; the eddies of bright sparks flew; and Kenelm was carried, whirling, on the moving air. When the air settled, there were three dead or dying men lying in golden light beside the fire, their throats torn and welling blood, their breath choking. Around them their friends were standing, turning every way, pointing, brandishing knives and calling out – but of the three women there was not a shadow.

Soon, though, from the darkness of the woods, the wolves sang. The men left by the fire dared not sit. Through all the long night, they stood, and marched around the fire's light, peering into the wood, where they saw, with every blink of their eyes, wolves, dark wolves, slipping from one darkness to the next.

At the first frail, grey light, the Foreigners ran away. They abandoned the sheep, they left their bundles, left everything except their shields and weapons, and they made for home. Kenelm, rising higher and ever higher into the air, like a hawk, looked down and watched them go, saw them make their way through the wood, and through the meadows beyond, and wade and swim across the river that made the border between his country and theirs.

Kenelm turned in the air, and was jolted by the hard, solid ground beneath him. The smell of crushed fern and grass rose about him. Opening his eyes he saw golden light and shadows – not sunlight and trees, but shifting firelight. There were voices. He was no longer in the wood. He closed his eyes again.

'Oh, how they ran!' Whispering laughter, and the whisper of a burning fire.

'Don't keep all of that for yourself, 'Runa.'

'Keep him warm! Cover him up!'

' 'Gifu's sitting nearest him – let her do it.'

Kenelm opened his eyes a little and looked about him with as little movement as possible. There was a wall behind him and on either side – flimsy walls of woven branches and leaves. He could hear, and feel, the breeze whisking through them. The roof above was rough thatch of fern over branches, while the front of the hut was open to the darkness and the wood. A fire burned at the opening, its flames leaping high, or flickering in the little breezes, and casting showers of red and golden sparks into the air. Its light lit a tangle of green and grey tree-trunks and branches, showing them in all their colour for a moment, and then letting them sink back into greys and darkness. The smell of the burning wood was both sharp and homely.

Between Kenelm and the fire sat the three Wood Women, still naked. The firelight cast a sheen over dark hair and shone on bare arms and legs. Kenelm closed his eyes as one turned towards him, and opened them carefully a moment later, when he could watch them without their knowing. They searched for lost apples among the grass and ferns on the floor of the hut, or ate berries gathered in a dish of bark; and they talked.

They weren't as alike as he'd thought. One he quickly judged to be the eldest – the others ducked their heads slightly when speaking to her, and asked her, 'What shall we do, 'Runa?' – the name meant 'counsel'. Her face had stillness and calm, and sharp, clear lines, as if it had been cut from stone.

The second of the women was plumper than the others, her face and smile softer and gentler, her breasts larger and her belly more curved. She was indolent, sprawling on the bedding and wriggling deeper into it. 'Wake up, 'Gifu,' the others said to her. 'We're speaking to you!' Gifu meant 'gift'.

The third woman had quick eyes, always sliding from one to another, eager to see the expression on a face. Several times she nearly caught Kenelm watching. Her smile was quick too, and more gleeful than kind. She was smaller than the others, her body wirier. 'Be quiet, 'Gara,' 'Runa said to her. 'Stop making trouble.' Gara meant 'spear'.

'He's awake,' said 'Gara, pointing a long thin arm and a long finger. 'He's watching us.'

'Gifu rolled over in the ferns, got to her knees and crawled to Kenelm's side. Kneeling beside him, she lifted up a wooden bowl and said, 'Drink some more of this. It tastes bad, but it'll cool the fever.'

He stared up at her. She was quite unconcerned that she was naked, and with her black hair falling down over her breasts, and her gentle smile, she was lovely. He couldn't think of offending her by refusing the bowl she offered – he would take the risk that she meant him harm. After all, they hadn't hurt him while he had been lying helpless. Rising on his elbow, he took the bowl and drank from it while looking up at her. The drink was cold and bitter, and he shuddered.

She smiled again, and put her hand on his head and stroked his hair. He was startled by her touch, but then delighted. He had been so many years in the monastery where no one had touched him at all. And now this beautiful woman touched him gently, lovingly. He was startled, shaken, by how much he had missed being touched. The other two women moved close, and he felt surrounded, protected. A strange tremulousness filled him, and his eyes welled with tears, surprising him.

'My name is Wulfgifu,' said the woman, stroking his head again. 'These are my sisters, Wulfruna and Wulfgara. We know your name. You're Kenelm.'

'Tell us about Egwin,' said Wulfruna.

'But drink first,' said Wulfgifu.

Kenelm took another mouthful of the bitter drink. 'He – he's one of the King's counsellors. An old man.'

'Oh! Has his face gone into folds and tucks?' Wulfgara pulled at her own face with her fingers, but it was too young to wrinkle.

'He is old,' Kenelm said, nodding.

Wulfruna hugged her knees. 'Such a pity to think . . . such a fine man, withering.' She shook her head. 'So sad.'

'You know Old Egwin?' Kenelm said.

Wulfruna turned her back on him, going back to the fire. A long, smooth back with a sweet groove running down its centre to a lovely swell of haunch. 'He was not old then.'

'You can tell Egwin, when you go back to him,' said Wulfgifu, 'that we did as he asked.'

'Tell him,' said Wulfgara, showing her white teeth, 'that we have hunted the Foreigners from his country!'

Wulfruna looked over her shoulder. 'Some have remained, but they'll claim only six feet of land.'

Wulfgifu smiled. 'But you need not fear wolves in the wood, Kenelm.'

'We won't bite *you*,' said Wulfgara, with her gleeful smile.

Kenelm feared that they *would* bite him – that they would kill him – but also felt an excited pleasure at the thought that, perhaps, he – he alone of all people – was safe with them. They were beautiful – the very thought of them would make the Christian monks sick with fury and loathing – and yet they granted him the privilege of being among them. He wanted urgently to escape from them, to be safe again – and he wanted to stay with them always, and have them touch his hair and stroke him.

'I have to go back,' he said. 'I have to take the news to my king.'

Wulfgifu lay down beside him and put her arms round him. 'Not yet. Not for days yet.'

'You couldn't walk a mile yet,' said Wulfruna.

'When you go,' said Wulfgara, 'you can take a

message from us. Tell them that we're coming to the feast.'

Kenelm frowned. 'The feast?'

Wulfgifu kissed him. 'The feast they're going to give to celebrate our victory.'

The other women laughed. Their dark eyes and white teeth shone in the firelight. 'On the night of the next full moon,' said Wulfruna.

'We've never been to a mortal feast before,' said Wulfgara. 'We want to hear the music!'

'See the dancing!'

'The men!' They laughed, a harsh, snapping, barking noise.

Kenelm laid his head down on his bed of ferns and saw stars shining through gaps in the thatch of fern above him.

Wulfgifu stretched herself beside him and her long hair fell over his chest and neck. He heard wolves howling, and saw a burning bear.

6

A proposal of marriage

Kenelm came through the trees, kicking through the leaves, and the swine raised their tails, grunted, and ran away from him. The boy herding them, running to head one off and turn it back towards the others, raised his switch and called, 'Good day!' Kenelm lifted his hand in reply.

He trudged on towards the Borough, and passed men mending field walls. Women in the fields were bending to glean the last grain. Coming near one party of men, Kenelm asked, 'How are things?' He was surprised to hear his own voice, surprised to feel it in his throat. It had been so long since he had spoken.

One of the men straightened from his work. 'Folk are getting back on their feet again, lord.'

'Some of 'em,' said another man.

'Good job the Foreigners didn't come visiting! There was nobody who could have done more than shout boo at 'em.'

'What d'you mean? My old gran could have shook her ladle at 'em. That'd have seen 'em off.'

Kenelm knew he was meant to be amused, and managed a half-hearted smile before going on towards the Borough's gate. The nearer he came to the gate, the more slowly he went, the more often he stopped. He even turned and looked back towards the woods.

He was glad, and proud, to be returning to the Borough with good news – but returning also meant a return to the grey, savourless life of the Christian brothers.

He thought of the firelight glowing over the rise of 'Runa's hip and along the length of her leg. 'Gifu had sat astride him and kissed him, her long hair falling about his face and shadowing him from the light. 'Gara had pulled his hair and stuck her tongue out at him.

They'd left him to rest in the shelter they'd built for him and gone out to hunt, coming back with

72

rabbits, with birds, even with a deer. For him, they roasted the meat, because he refused to eat it raw. They cared for him, with gentleness and kindness, though he knew they were neither gentle nor kind. He was nervous with them, but when they bit or scratched, it was only in play, and it made him feel wonderfully safe and protected – they could hurt him, but they wouldn't. Not him.

He looked down the years stretching ahead of him in the monastery – long, lonely years, without their warm company, their beauty – without the world – and it was as if he looked down an endless, narrow, cold corridor of grey stone while, behind him, a heavy door slammed.

Unhappiness weighed him down so that he was pressed to the ground and he sat, not caring about the mud. He only wanted to get to his feet again to walk back to the woods, back to 'Gifu and 'Runa and 'Gara ... but he was of the Royal Kin, an atheling, Woden-born, and it was his duty to bring the news back to the Borough. It was his duty to go back to the monastery, because he had been given to the monks by his uncle, the King, and he had to honour the King's gift.

He sat there, his face in his hands, seesawing

between what he wanted to do and what he ought to do, until he became aware that the day was passing and the wind was cold. Gritting his teeth, he made himself get up and trudged through the gates, into the Borough, with his news.

Egwin was in bed, half-sitting and half-lying, propped up with many pillows and cushions. The window-shutters were open, and the day's light came in through the panes of scraped horn. A wood fire in an iron brazier released a scent of apple-wood, and warmed the room. His eyes closed, Egwin listened to the bard who sat beside his bed, softly singing 'The Wood Woman's Lament'.

> ' *"When I was young and foolish –*
> *A thousand years ago –*
> *I loved a mortal man,*
> *And mortal proved his love.*
> *He said that he would love me*
> *A thousand years, a thousand years,*
> *But one glimpse of my hollow back*
> *And in an eye's blink,*
> *An eye's-blink,*
> *His love was gone . . ."* '

74

The singer stopped short at a knock at the room's door, and looked at Egwin to see what he should do.

'Answer it, if you would be so kind,' Egwin said. 'Save me from raising my voice.'

The bard rose, carrying his lyre, and went to open the door, where he exchanged a few quiet words with someone outside. Coming back to the bed, he said, 'Kenelm Atheling has returned, my lord, and asks if he might speak with you.'

'Kenelm!' said the old man. 'Yes! Have him sent to me at once - and you, you may go. But tell the servants to bring wine and food.'

There were still sick people lying wrapped in blankets on the floor of the hall, but many fewer than there had been. A steward had greeted Kenelm as he entered the hall, though the man looked drawn and tired, and a serving man had brought him a horn of ale as he waited to hear if Egwin would see him. Another servant escorted him through the hall to the door of Egwin's private room.

Kenelm was struck, as he entered, by the room's warmth and stuffiness, but was also reminded of his own grubbiness. The room was swept and clean, and the old man sitting up in the bed wore a linen shirt, and his long hair and beard were sleek from combing. Kenelm, putting up a hand to his own tangled hair, found leaves and bits of twig. 'Forgive me, Master Egwin, for not staying to wash and change before coming to you. I wanted to give you my news at once.'

'Water will be brought soon,' the old man said. 'You may wash your hands and face then. On top of that chest you'll find a comb. Take a seat and – ask after my health.'

Kenelm shook his head. There was, he felt, no time for small talk. Opening the pouch that hung at his belt, he took out the token he'd been given, and passed it to the old man. Egwin, reaching for it, saw that it was a wild rose, one of the last of the year. It was wilted now, but the flat, pale pink flower, with the crown of gold stamens at the centre, gave off a faint, sweet scent. 'From Wulfruna,' the old man said.

'She made me promise to give it to you.'

'A thousand thanks to you,' said the old man, and fell silent. Kenelm, watching, saw a slow tear spill from his sagging lid on to the folds and bags beneath his eye.

For a long time, Egwin looked at the flower, fingering its spray of sharp green leaves, touching the satin of the petals, sniffing it. There was a knock on the door, it was opened, and servants came in,

76

the first carrying a ewer of hot water, a bowl and a towel; the second bearing a tray with a wine jug and cups; and the third a tray of wheat cakes. They set all these things down on the chests that stood against the wall, and quickly left again.

Egwin, still holding the rose, said, 'What is she like now?'

Kenelm sat on the edge of the bed. 'So beautiful. Hair as black as . . . polished coal. Soft as thistledown. Eyes so big and white and black, they swallow you. Beautiful.' I must go back to them, he thought. I can't live on for years without them. I don't care what is said or thought of me.

'And young?' said the old man.

'Younger than me.'

The old man sighed, and fell silent.

'They drove away the Foreigners,' Kenelm said. 'Drove them as wolves drive sheep or deer. I don't think they'll be eager to come back to our haunted woods.' I have to stay, he thought. This is my country and these are my people. I can't leave. If it's thought best for me to work for them from a monastery, well then, that's the lot fallen to me.

'Good,' said the old man. 'Good. I knew they would help us.' His eyes left his flower again and sent a darting look at Kenelm. 'So. You found the Wood Women beautiful?'

Kenelm struggled to keep his face blank and hoped he was succeeding. 'No one could look at them and say they were not beautiful. But . . . but it wouldn't be wise to dwell on their beauty, I think.'

'It would not,' Egwin said, his eyes returning to his flower. 'I shouldn't have sent you to them. Your abbot – there was the man to send. A man not subject to the beauty of women – and certainly not Wood Women. But the abbot is a Christian and not to be trusted. Everyone else I could trust was sick. I should never have sent you otherwise.'

Kenelm went over to the chest and washed his hands, drying them on the towel the servant had left. He filled a cup with wine, and brought it and the plate of cakes to the old man. 'Master Egwin, may I ask you a question?'

'Certainly you may.'

'You are not a Christian, are you?'

The old man gave a laugh and shook his head.

'And my uncle, the King – he is not a Christian?'

'You hardly need to ask these questions.'

'Then why must I be a Christian?'

'A matter of statecraft,' the old man said. 'The Christians are no great power in our land as yet – but they are in lands to the south of us, and it may be their power will grow here. We – the King needs a reliable man among them, to learn their ways and their thinking, and to tell us of them. And to speak for us among them.'

Kenelm filled himself a cup, and sat on the chest. He took a deep drink. 'So I am to be the reliable man?'

'One of the Royal Kin,' Egwin said. 'An atheling, who will be loyal to his Kin above all.'

'I never wanted to become a monk, Master Egwin, ever.'

'Your uncle didn't want to become king, but the Council chose him from among the Kin. When Woden planted His seed here on Earth, to begin your line, this is what He planted you for. Do you break your back in the fields every day? No. Do you wear one thin tunic winter and summer? No, you are well supplied with shirts and robes, stockings, boots and cloaks: you need never shiver. And, tell me, are you the first or the last to go hungry when food is short?'

There was a pause while the old man frowned, waiting for a meek answer.

'Master Egwin,' Kenelm said, 'I can tell you know little about the life of a monk. I am always hungry. In winter, I'm always cold. I am always digging.'

Egwin was annoyed. 'No matter. The task of the Royal Kin is to do all that they may to keep peace and order in the kingdom, and it ill becomes them to shirk that task.'

'Let someone else be my uncle's monk,' Kenelm said.

Egwin sipped his wine. 'That would take many more years. You are almost a monk already.'

Kenelm's head hung. But I don't want to be a monk, he thought. I want to wear bright colours and gold rings. And hunt. And drink and feast. I want to marry.

'The King is up and about again,' Egwin said. 'Come to night-meal in the hall tonight. You'll have a seat at the high-table, and can make your report to your uncle yourself. I'm sure he'll reward you.'

The only reward I want is to be freed from my vows, Kenelm thought. I should run away. I must run away . . . But if he did, he would be ungrateful, a shirker, a coward. A traitor.

King Adhelm's hall was long and high, the timber arches of the roof lost in shadows. Around the walls hung beautiful, costly hangings, embroidered in bright colours, with gold and silver threads glittering in the stitching. One showed the three Gods, Woden, Loki and Heimdall, creating the first man from an ash tree, and the first woman from an elm; another showed Woden attending the birth of the first of King Adhelm's line, and driving His gift of a magic sword into the house-tree.

The body of the hall was occupied by long tables. At the lowest, furthest from the heat and light of the fire, the lesser members of the household – kennelmen and grooms, swineherds and henwives – ate while standing. At the higher tables sat the young men of the King's bodyguard, who laughed, yelled, banged on the tables with their fists, slopped ale about and threw bread at each other. The whole hall resounded with noise and movement – not only chatter and laughter, but the drowsy twitterings of birds perched in the rafters, the clashing of ladles on the sides of vessels, the shouting of toasts and orders, the hurrying to and fro of servants with food and drink.

The King's high table was set across the hall, at right angles to the others, and the fire burned before it, the light glittering on the gold and silver that trimmed the drinking-horns, on the golden pins in the Queen's headdress, and on the brooches at the shoulders of her blue dress. Adhelm, too, wore a circlet in his hair, bracelets on his wrists and rings on his fingers. His tunic was a rich scarlet. The salt, placed before him on the table, was held in a shining golden bowl.

Kenelm sat at the end of the high table, saddened by all he saw and heard. He looked at the bright colours about him, at the glitter of precious metals and jewels, and thought of the drab grey stone and drab grey and brown robes of the monastery to which he would soon be returning. He tasted the good food, the fish and the meat, with the delicate sauces flavoured with saffron and almonds, and drank the wine served with it, and thought of the monastery's dull, plain meals. In place of this lively noise and laughter, the monastery had silence. And in the monastery the women did not wear bright colours and sit laughing with their hair streaming loose over their shoulders. How can I, he thought, return to the monastery and continue to merely peep across the dining hall at the dowdy nuns? If I have to go back there, I shall do something mad. I shall *go* mad.

'A toast to Kenelm!' King Adhelm yelled out. His voice rose easily over the hubbub – he was used to making himself heard. 'To Kenelm, who braved the ghosts and creatures of the deep woods, to save our hides from the Foreigners! Kenelm!'

A shattering roar of, 'Kenelm!' roused the birds from the rafters and set them fluttering, feathers drifting down through the air. Kenelm, startled despite himself, jumped, and blushed.

'Stand up, stand up!' Adhelm roared. 'Tell us about your journey.'

'Tell us about the Wood Women!' someone bawled from among the bodyguard.

Kenelm stood, and the cheers and applause rose, before falling silent as the whole assembly waited to hear what he would say. The silence drew out, as they waited, and Kenelm tried to find words.

'There's little to tell, King,' he said, at last. 'I did as Lord Egwin told me.' He knew he was disappointing everyone. They wanted to hear an exciting tale, well-told, not these lame words. 'I went deep into the wood and broke a tree. The Wood Women came to me then.'

From the body of the hall came whistles and cheers.

Kenelm raised his voice. 'They were fine ladies.' He knew that this called up a picture of women like the Queen and princesses, dressed in linen, gold and garnets, rather than the wild, naked hoydens he'd seen – but he had no wish to share what he had seen with everyone gathered in the hall, especially not with the whooping bodyguards. 'As soon as I appealed to them for help, they granted it.'

Kenelm could see his uncle, the King, looking at him along the table. Adhelm pulled a face, meaning: Spice it up a little; give them something worth listening to.

'I can tell you little else,' Kenelm said. 'I fell sick, and was left behind when the three ladies went to battle . . .' He had no intention of describing how the lovely women had shrugged themselves into wolf-shapes. It seemed indelicate. Nor did he want to tell how they lulled the Foreigners into dropping their guard. He didn't want to set the bodyguards whooping again. 'They came back to me when they had driven the Foreigners off, and—'

A roar of sound rose from the body of the hall, as people yelled and laughed, beat fists on the tables, whistled, cheered. 'Drove them off! Drove the Foreigners off! Made 'em run, sent 'em packing!' The din, echoing among the rafters, disturbed roosting birds.

Kenelm, finding his words drowned beneath the din, stood, waiting. The noise dropped as the people seemed to tire, and he took a breath and opened his mouth, ready to speak again – but the people rallied and raised the hullaballoo again. It dipped and rose several more times, before silence fell.

Kenelm cleared his throat. 'They nursed me with great kindness,' he said, embarrassed, but determined to get through his little speech. 'Until I was well enough to make my way back here. Where I am glad to be again.'

Another cheer was raised, though it was much more half-hearted, and died away more quickly. Still Kenelm remained standing. King Adhelm peered at him along the length of the table, frowned and nodded for him to sit down.

'I have another message to deliver,' Kenelm said. 'A message from the Wood Women. At the next full moon they will come here. They ask that we give a feast for them. To celebrate their victory.'

There were no cheers. Instead a deep silence spread throughout the hall, reaching to the furthest corners. It seemed to Kenelm, as he stood at the high table that, despite the nearness of the fire, a slight chill breeze reached him. It was fear, the superstitious fear of everyone gathered under the hall's roof, at the thought of these Wood Beings, these shadow-dwellers, night-comers, coming among them.

King Adhelm said, 'They will be welcome! They gave us their help generously, when we needed it, and we shall thank them as generously. The long-fires shall be lit! The tables shall be spread! The horns shall be filled with wine and mead!'

Now the cheers rose again. They always did, for the King. Adhelm waited until the noise had almost died, and then stilled it with a gesture. 'We will welcome our friends and allies, the Ladies of the Wood, with precious gifts. For, says the poet, "There is no one who will not return thanks for good gifts given."

'And, should we need the help of the Wood Folk again, they will hurry to our aid, bound to us by gratitude!'

More cheers. While the noise went on, the King turned to his Queen and daughters, as if about to ask them what they thought the Wood Women would like as gifts. But, before he spoke, he paused, became thoughtful, and squinted at the fire's flames for a while. 'Better still,' he said, 'to bind them close in alliance, so that our good is their good. I shall find them husbands!'

Stillness fell on the hall again. The Queen said, 'Marry one of our men to a – Wood Woman?'

Into the silence of his watching, listening men, the King said, 'It would bring honour to our house and to theirs. It will attest our gratitude better than any gift. It will strengthen us – and them!'

The Queen turned her face away from him, her expression bewildered.

Kenelm spoke. In the quiet he was easily heard. 'King. Uncle. May I ask a favour?'

Adhelm turned towards him, frowning slightly. 'Ask!'

Kenelm wanted to insist on the King agreeing to grant him whatever he asked before he asked it, as heroes did in stories. But Adhelm would be furious if he tried such a trick, and he didn't dare. 'King. I . . . I am of the Royal Kin. I wish to be married. Marry *me* to the Wood Women. To one of them. To Wulfgifu.'

King Adhelm looked at him as if he didn't understand the language he was speaking. 'What?'

'Nothing but good can come of an alliance with the Wood Women,' Kenelm called out. He was conscious of the rapt attention from the lower tables, and he felt heat in his face. 'Let me make the match for our side. Let me marry one of the Wood Women.'

Adhelm's frown deepened and he shook his head slightly. 'You're the Christian!'

'King – Uncle – I never chose to be a Christian! I don't want to be a monk. Release me from the monastery! I can be of more use to you if–'

'Of what use to me is a man who's never held a sword and shield? You're trained as a monk; you shall *be* a monk.' Kenelm opened his mouth to speak, and Adhelm scowled. 'Don't argue! Sit down! You shall go back to your Christians tomorrow, by Father Woden you shall!' Kenelm still stood, staring. 'Did you hear me? Sit!'

Slowly, Kenelm sat. He looked at the cooling food on his plate – such good food, so well-cooked and delicately flavoured – while the noise of talk and laughter rose around him again. Excited talk, discussing which of the athelings would be offered in marriage to the Wood Women. And would any of them dare to marry with such a creature? But would they dare disobey Aldhelm?

Kenelm ate nothing more. His thoughts were full of the monastery's whitewashed walls, the endless praying, the scant food, the nuns in their limp grey robes and their covered hair. Images of Wulfgifu, Wulfruna and Wulfgara kept creeping in, but they were drowned and lost in the grey, dreary cold of monastery life that was going to be his life, all his life. His unlife.

7

The feast at full moon

First, the hall was swept. A party of maids with brooms set to work, sweeping up the old straw and herbs covering the floor, swept it all out of the door and into the yard, together with ash and old bones and bits of dropped, stale bread.

Next, the wall-hangings were to be taken down. They had been hanging for many months and had been grimed by smoke from the fire. It wasn't an easy job. The hangings were weighty squares of wool, made weightier with the close stitching of their embroidery, and the gold and silver thread that glittered in them. The servants climbed ladders, balancing awkwardly on the rungs, struggling with the sagging folds as they lowered them into the arms of other servants below. The dust that escaped in clouds from the thick cloth made everyone who came near cough.

Other, even finer hangings, taken from store, were hung in their place, meaning more struggles and more coughing. But when the work was done, the freshness of the unfamiliar hangings made the hall look even bigger and grander, and everyone, servants and masters, stood for a while to admire the effect. But soon the maids were chivvied back to work. They fetched fresh straw, mixed with dried lavender and other sweet-scented herbs, and strewed the floor with it.

The long trestle tables were set up, running the length of the hall and, because this feast would be for nobles only, the tables were covered with cloths of yellow, blue and red, and benches were set beside the tables. At each place was set a drinking horn, its rim decorated with shining metal, and a spoon of polished horn.

The high table where the King and Queen would sit had been covered with a white cloth, and the bowl of salt, at its centre, was of shining gold. Here there were no mere benches, but two large, armed chairs for the royal couple, and stools at the other places. The horns were marvellous shining things made out of glass, with metal stands to hold them upright, so they did not have to be emptied before they could be set down. The spoons were of silver-gilt.

Down the length of the hall, between the tables, the long fires had been lit, blazing and filling the building with golden light and heat. The light shimmered over the gold, glinted on gold and silver threads in the wall-hangings, and flickered among the beams high above in the roof, where sleepy, disturbed birds chirruped. The heat brought the scent of wood from the walls, and of old grass from the thatch.

Kenelm saw the hall when he entered with the other guests, all nobles, all dressed in bright colours, with gold necklaces, armbands and belt-buckles. There were many women, who would not sit at the tables, but at the benches along the walls, behind their men. Kenelm watched them as they moved to their places, or greeted each other. The young, unmarried daughters had loose hair streaming over their shoulders – it looked so soft and shining – or bound into thick plaits woven with coloured ribbons. Their waists were girdled with coloured cords or belts of shining metallic links. The married women – many of whom were also young and pretty – had their hair gathered under linen hoods. Only their husbands – their lucky husbands, who had not been handed over to Christian monks – could see or touch their hair.

He had been loitering about the court for more than a week, waiting for this night, the night of the Full-Moon Feast. It had been a nervous wait – at every moment he had expected to be called into his uncle's presence and asked why he hadn't returned to the monastery – or told that the Abbot, or Lady Abbess had sent messengers enquiring about his whereabouts. But no one sent for him. It seemed he was not important enough to be remembered.

It wasn't difficult to live unnoticed at the court. Within the walls of the Royal Borough were many halls where a warm, dry place to sleep could be found, and many halls where all comers were fed, morning and evening. There were so many servants, and soldiers, and animal herds and workers of all descriptions, all coming and going, that no one took much notice of one more man, even if he *was* dressed like a Christian monk. It was assumed that he had business with someone.

And, within three days, Kenelm had learned that

his eldest brother, Cuthman, was staying at the Borough, in their family's hall. Kenelm went to him and admitted that he was playing truant from the monastery, because he wanted to see the feast.

Cuthman promised that he wouldn't give Kenelm away, but only after Kenelm gave his word that, once the feast was over, he would return to the monastery. There was no harm, Cuthman said, in having a little fun – especially when what Kenelm told him of the monastery sounded so grim – but he couldn't be part of Kenelm breaking his vows. That would be a disgrace to the whole family.

'*I* never made any vows,' Kenelm said.

'No matter. Our father and uncle made them for you. You'll disgrace them if you go back on your word.'

'It's easy for you to speak high-mindedly,' Kenelm said. 'It's not you that has to be a monk.'

'If I had been vowed to the monastery,' Cuthman said, 'I would be a monk. I would be the best monk I could be.'

Hearing this, Kenelm had gritted his teeth, and longed to deny it, but couldn't. He had no doubt that, in his place, Cuthman would set himself to be the most pious, the most self-sacrificing, the most righteous and holy man in the monastery – a champion monk. In fact, all around him were dutiful people putting their utmost into doing what they had to do. It was only he who grudged the effort.

'Well, you can't go about dressed like that,' Cuthman said, nodding at Kenelm's grey habit. 'I'll find you out some clothes.' Kenelm's hopes rose, but Cuthman refused to part with any of his finery. He gave Kenelm an old red shirt which washing had made baggy and had faded to a colour like much-watered wine; a pair of blue breeches, also faded, pale, and baggy at the knee; and leather shoes, scuffed and worn, but fastened with golden acorns. The belt round his waist was of plain leather, unornamented, with a simple iron buckle, and a small iron knife with a bone handle. The band to hold back his hair was plain blue, without embroidery. He looked shabby – more like some impoverished thane who shared his hall with his animals than an atheling – but at least he drew no curious glances.

Servants – many of them wearing better clothes than Kenelm – were greeting the guests as they entered the hall, and leading the more noble to their places at the higher tables. Kenelm ducked behind a family party and made his own way to the lower tables at the far end of the hall. It was a place that suited his clothes, and was as far as he could get from the high table and the eyes of his uncle, the King, and his aunt, the Queen.

The flames of the long-fire burned in front of him, leaping, gauzy, yellow flames, throwing off sparks and little snatches of fire that quickly died in the air. On the further side of the flames were the tables on the opposite side of the hall, and the men seating themselves there, in their bright tunics and headbands, with flashing brooches at their shoulders and rings on their fingers. Behind them, between their heads and over their shoulders, he could catch glimpses of their wives and daughters. And soon he would see again Wulfgifu, and Wulfruna, and Wulfgara. If they came. If they kept their promise and really came.

The clamour of many people taking all at once was pierced by the high sound of trumpets, silencing everyone. After the scream of the trumpets died away, the birds in the rafters could be heard shifting, flapping wings and chirping. At the lower end of the hall, people were standing, the better to see. Kenelm rose with them, and saw the King and Queen arriving, both dressed in red with gold circlets on their heads. They took their seats, and the more important princelings and courtiers took their places

97

at the ends of the table. Old Egwin was among them, seemingly weighed down by his robes, and helped to his stool by a servant. The most honoured seats, those next to the King – the places where the Wood Women would sit – remained empty.

Servants hurried about the hall with towels over their arms, carrying bowls of water to the tables for the guests to wash their hands. Male servants waited on the men, and women waited on the ladies who sat against the wall. Before the wash-basins had reached the hall's lower end, the horns were being filled with feast-ale at the upper end. The King, rising to his feet, and holding his shining glass drinking horn high in the air, filled his lungs and bellowed, 'Wassail, wassail, good friends!'

In a deafening shout, like a blow to the ears, every man in the hall bawled back, 'Drinkheil! Drinkheil!' and then burst into laughter. The noise disturbed the birds in the rafters again.

Servants hurried about the hall again, carrying loaves and knives. Pausing at each place they cut a thick slice of bread from their loaves and set it before the guest as his trencher, on which his food would be served. The slice set before Kenelm had been coloured green, with parsley.

All around was a susurration of voices, sometimes

rising in a sharp burst of chatter or of laughter. Everyone was questioning whether the Wood Women would come – whether they would dare to come – whether anyone in the hall could face them. And what would they be like – did they have backs like rotten, hollow trees, as the stories said? Would they bless or curse? The people near Kenelm had other considerations too: what would the food be? Would there be plenty of drink? Would there be singers, dancers, jugglers?

'It's been so long since I heard music,' said a woman somewhere behind him. 'I do hope there's music.'

Only Kenelm was thinking solely of the Wood Women. Only he knew how beautiful they were. His heart slowly increased its beat as he thought of them, until it was thumping hard and heavy in his chest. He pressed his hands against the table, took deep breaths and calmed himself – but immediately his thoughts were with the Wood Women again, and his heart started its fast beating again at the idea that they might not come.

But they would . . . They must . . . Around him the women were dressed in blue, in yellow, in red. Some of the richer ones wore silk. But the Wood Women – they would come dressed in cloth of gold . . . In silver cloth woven from spider's silk, and jewelled with flowers. Their gowns would flow like shining liquid and everyone's mouths would drop open in amazement. Their dark hair would fall over their shoulders and breasts – no. It would be plaited and every plait would be hung with golden apples and silver birds . . . They would have gold at their necks, at their wrists and fingers, at their waists . . . And, like the Goddess Freya's golden girdle, their jewels would make them twice as beautiful as they were. No one in the hall would be able to look away from them. And, in front of everyone, he would rise from his seat and go forward to greet them, and they would take his hands and kiss him . . .

The trumpets sounded again, and again silence fell over the hall. But this time, when people stood, it was with more eagerness than before. They jumped up, gasping and already craning their necks to see. Kenelm felt his heart almost stop with excitement. He could hardly draw breath and, as he tried to stand, his knees threatened to buckle. They had come! Wulfgifu, Wulfruna, Wulfgara – they were here!

He tried to see, but there were too many heads bobbing into his way, arms being raised to point. Kenelm clambered on to his stool and saw, through the smoke, that the Wood Women had come and were walking up the hall, beside the flames of the long-fire, towards the high table.

Their long dark hair fell over their shoulders and down to their waists. It shone in the firelight like smooth, dark glass. They wore no gold ornaments in their hair – instead each wore a spray of brilliant red berries and a red-gold leaf. And, beside these leaves and berries, and their long hair, they wore nothing but their wolf-skins. As they walked away from him, he saw the grey pelts hanging from their shoulders, and their long bare legs and bare feet beneath. They walked as if they wore silk – as if they wore crowns.

The crowd in the feast hall watched them in silence. There was no ribaldry, nor any whistles or hisses. The onlookers were, Kenelm realised, afraid.

The Wood Women reached the high table. The King came forward and embraced them, and kissed them on the cheek. If anyone in the hall thought that Adhelm was lucky, no one dared to say so, or to cheer, and the King himself behaved as if greeting naked women was nothing out of the way. He handed the women on to his Queen, who kissed them herself, before leading them to the stools that had been set for them. Kenelm, watching, thought that old Egwin would greet them but instead the old man turned his face aside and looked away from them. The three women seemed not to notice him at all. They sat, and then the other guests sat too, and the Wood Women looked about them curiously, smiling, their bare arms catching the light and their breasts peeking from their dark falls of hair. Kenelm realised that they did not recognise Egwin. They had known him as a young man – and old Egwin, who was still refusing to look at them, was ashamed of his shrunken frame, his grey hair and wrinkled face. A pang of pity struck under Kenelm's breastbone, and a voice whispered in his ear: If you go with them, this is what you can expect.

An unusual silence still hung over the hall. No one dared to look at his or her neighbour, or to whisper anything of what they might be thinking. But Kenelm thought he could hear their thoughts, and he stared about him, glared almost, ready to shout down the first man who dared to say anything unkind about the Wood Women.

The Queen rose and beckoned to a servant who hurried to bring her a small bucket of polished wood staves, bound with shining metal. From this bucket, with a gleaming ladle, the Queen measured mead into the glass horns in front of her guests, straining it through the small gilded strainer which hung from her girdle.

King Adhelm lifted his own glass horn and shouted, so that the whole hall could hear, 'We, the sons of Woden, give welcome to the People of the Wood! Wassail!'

Back came the answering roar: 'Drinkheil!'

One of the Wood Women, the one seated in the middle, rose to her feet. They were so much alike that Kenelm, watching from the other end of the hall, through the uncertain light and shifting smoke, could not tell which one she was. She lifted the shining glass horn of mead with both hands, holding it high in front of her. Her dark hair was pushed back and fell behind her, and her breasts rose. Every man in the hall was silent, gaping. Nor did any of the women so much as whisper.

'Be in good health!' the Wood Woman cried, and Kenelm knew by her voice that it was Wulfruna.

'Health!' came an answering roar from the body of the hall, with a din that lifted into the rafters and shook dust down into the firelight.

The trumpets sounded again, and servants brought the first course to the tables. Reluctantly, people got down from the benches and returned to their seats, unwilling to lose sight of the Wood Women, but equally unwilling to miss the food.

People were still standing on the benches when Kenelm got down. He wanted to go on gazing at the Wood Women, but didn't want to make himself conspicuous. On the table before him was set white bread, and dishes of butter and soft cheese. It was all excellent, the bread fine and soft, with a crisp crust, the butter rich, the cheese with a salty tang. At the high table, there was probably fruit too. Kenelm ate greedily, thinking of the tough, dark, heavy bread at the monastery, with its scant scraping of butter. He could not go back: he could not.

The trumpets rang out, and the servants went about the hall again, filling horns with drink, this time with sweet mead. King Adhelm rose and lifted his glass horn again. 'Ladies of the Wood, I drink to you and pledge you friendship!' From the hall rose a cheer that agreed with him.

The Queen rose and, with wide, dramatic gestures so that everyone could see what she was doing, stripped from her fingers three gold rings. These she presented to the Wood sisters. 'May the friendship between us,' bellowed King Adhelm, 'be as endless as these rings and as incorruptible!'

The sisters rose and accepted the rings. The one nearest to the Queen – whether it was Wulfgifu or

Wulfgara, Kenelm couldn't tell – kissed her cheek in thanks, her wild hair tumbling across the Queen's silken clothes; and the two further from her kissed their fingers in token of thanks. All gathered in the hall cheered again, and cheered until the whole great wooden hall seemed to shudder.

The servants were running about in the din, serving the second course, the course of delicacies. On to Kenelm's trencher was served a meat pudding in a suet crust, with slices of spicy sausage around it. The scented steam rising from it filled his mouth with water, and all around him people were eating eagerly, but after his first two mouthfuls, appetite rapidly left him. He stared down the length of the hall at the three dark-haired Wood Women. His uncle would present them with gifts, as was the custom. Among those gifts would be husbands. But he would not be one of them.

As the last of the meat puddings were being scraped from the plates, a lyre, decorated with mother-of-pearl and gold, was brought to King Adhelm, who stood and struck its strings. The din of talk and laughter died to a hush. They might have gone on chattering through the playing of another minstrel, but this was the King.

The King sang in praise of the Wood Women,

beautiful and courageous, who came to the aid of the sons of Woden and drove away the Foreigners . . . Kenelm didn't think it very good, even if it had been improvised on the spot – which it wasn't likely to have been. Everyone practised their 'improvised' feast-songs for days.

When the King struck a chord on the lyre again, and set it down on the table, applause roared the length of the hall, with everyone trying to shout and clap louder than anyone else, to show their loyalty and love. Kenelm patted his hands together, so he wouldn't draw attention to himself, but he felt no enthusiasm.

Trumpets blared and the servants ran about the hall with the third course: poached cod in a thick pottage of spiced vegetables, while the horns were filled with red wine brought, expensively, from the continent. Kenelm could not touch any of it, and was forced to sit holding the horn of wine, which he could not set down without spilling, until his neighbour was ready to take it from him and drink it. Kenelm was held by the sight of one of the Wood Women rising to her feet. She held out her hands for the lyre, and the King passed it to her.

A hush fell throughout the hall as the woman took the lyre. She settled it into her arm, and her hand dawdled over the strings, plucking from them a spatter of sound, like scattering raindrops, of such sweetness that the hush became utter silence.

All the stories said, Kenelm remembered, with open mouth, that the Wood Folk had an uncanny talent for music.

The woman shook back her thick dark hair, uncovering one full round breast to the firelight, and she sang. Then Kenelm was certain that it was Wulfgifu, and his attention became so fixed that he was no longer aware of himself standing in the hall, but only of her.

'We bless the Master of this house,
The Mistress also.
And all the little childer that round the table go.
We bless the hearth, the barn, the byre,
The dog outside the door.
We bless whate'er you have in store
And send you ten times more.'

Wulfgifu's voice, deep and sweet and dark as honey, reached out to every corner of the hall, holding on to long, high notes and long, deep notes until they died away so exquisitely, it wrang the heart. And when everyone was thinking – they could almost be

107

felt thinking – that this was the loveliest music they had ever heard, two other voices joined the singing, both higher, coiling and shifting about the notes of Wulfgifu's voice, until the hair of the listeners prickled and lifted with the eeriness of beauty.

The song ended with another shaking of water-drops from the lyre, and the silence in the hall was like a blow. It went on and on, the men and women crowded into the hall too awestruck to make a movement or a whisper or a sigh. And when they did stir, and turn to each other with astonished faces, still the silence went on, for a deep peace had settled over the hall. All felt it, and none wished to disturb it.

Wulfgifu smiled, set the lyre on the table, and sat. At the other end of the hall Kenelm didn't so much sit as drop on to his seat. His eyes were stinging and blurred with tears, and tears filled his throat.

The silence might have gone on another hour if King Adhelm hadn't shaken himself and pointed to the trumpeters, who blew their trumpets to announce the next and final course. The servants carried round basins of a thick, smooth paste made from boiled wheat, mixed with honey, almonds and fruit; and the horns were filled with more mead. All around the hall men rose and, yelling to shake the roof-timbers, toasted the Wood Women.

The cheering went on and on, even after King Adhelm had risen and lifted his arms above his head. The King stood still, holding his arms high and, slowly, the cheering quietened. Raising his voice, to be heard above the last of the din, Adhelm said, 'A King must reward a sweet singer – what shall be the gift? Gold is precious, but hard and cold – yet what is worth more than gold?' He turned and looked at his guests. 'What, to a beautiful woman, is worth more than gold?' Smiling, he turned to face the hall. He stretched out his arm, from which folds of silken sleeve fell and on which gold bands glistened. He beckoned.

In the body of the hall, three figures rose from the seats nearest the high table. They stepped into the light of the fire, and of the candles that burned about the most honoured guests. They were all tall young men, all dressed in bright colours, with embroidered borders to their tunics, and headbands tied about their fair hair, and jewellery of amber, gold and garnets. The cheering began again as the youths arranged themselves in a row in front of the high table. Kenelm, standing for a better view, recognised them as three of his cousins, all nephews of the King and athelings like himself, members of the Royal Kin.

His fists clenched as he looked at them. He wished he had a weapon in his grip – an axe, a club. Why were they so favoured? Why was happiness being gifted to them? Then he saw the Wood Women.

They had risen from their seats, all three together. They were standing at the high table, on its dais raised above the body of the hall, and he could see them clearly over the heads of the three young athelings. The women were standing tall and straight, stiff with anger. Their eyes were staring and bright, their brows frowning, their mouths tight. It was as if a wind blew from them, buffeting the faces of those watching. Kenelm wanted to take a step back.

King Adhelm was not looking at the Wood Women, but at his audience in the hall and at his nephews, the athelings. 'Love, to a woman, is worth more than gold. I give you, each of you, a husband to serve and to love, a husband who will serve and cherish you – each one of the line of Woden. An alliance that will bind us—'

Those in the body of the hall could see the Wood Women. The cheering wavered uncertainly, and died. The King's voice rang suddenly loud. Startled, he hesitated, looked round, and saw the Wood Women.

'That will bind us,' he said again, but his voice had lost its confidence. 'That will . . .' He stopped.

The Wood Women did not move or speak. The three athelings looked at each other, and two of them half-turned, as if to go back to their seats, but then looked at their uncle. Receiving no sign from him, they stayed where they were.

In the hall, people who had been standing to see better now cringed back into their seats. They looked away from the scene, at the table-top, at the floor. Women along the benches hid their heads under their shawls.

Kenelm remained on his feet, watching and waiting, open mouthed. The fire-light and shadows rolling about the hall seemed like the rolling of thunder-clouds, the dimness like the dimness of storm light.

Wulfruna spoke. 'Vermin.' Then she and her sisters broke from their stillness. They snatched up their wolf-skins from their seats, leaped from the dais and strode for the door. As they went, they pulled at their fingers and, tugging off the rings, hurled them at the floor, sending them bouncing and rolling away under the tables.

The athelings shrank back and let them by. Those seated at the tables watched them approach, and watched them pass by, but ducked their heads when they were near, afraid to meet their eyes. The guards at the door made no attempt to stop them – and the doors sprang open with a creaking of wood and iron as they drew near.

As Kenelm watched, they were gone – gone into the darkness outside. Inside him, his heart seemed to cry out: Come back! But he didn't move.

'Move!' It was King Adhelm's voice, startling everyone. Kenelm flinched as if he'd been struck. It was as if he'd been asleep and dreaming, and the King's voice had shaken him awake. Around the hall he saw many others starting, and staring round with open mouths and wide eyes.

'Go after them!' The King was shouting at the guards. 'Move, you blockheads! Bring them back!' The King's face was red, his eyes bulging. 'Get them!'

The guards plunged outside, and many others, jumping up from the tables, followed them. Kenelm ran after them, but stopped short in the chill of the yard, his eyes blinded by the darkness after the dazzle of firelight. Around him he heard men shouting, and glimpsed faint shapes lunging this way and that.

Standing in the cold yard, Kenelm started to laugh. No one would catch the Wood Women, he knew that. They were already far away, running not on two feet, but on four.

8

The abbess

'They called me vermin!' King Adhelm was in council in his hall. He glared at old Egwin who sat next to him, and then, leaning forward over his knees, glowered at the other lords and athelings gathered about him. 'Insulted my nephews – insulted my blood! Threw my gold in my teeth!'

A ripple of movement passed through the crowd: a murmuring, a whispering, an angry rustling. Much time, wealth and labour had been expended to honour the Wood Women, and the ingratitude stung. Kenelm, at the back of the crowd, felt the anger creeping, unwanted, into his own nerves.

Old Egwin, a heap of furs in a high-backed wooden chair, spoke. 'My lord King: be mindful that they are not of our kind. They are Wood Folk.'

'I know what they are!'

Egwin raised frail, bony hands and waved them, dismissing the King's ill-temper. 'Their ways are not our ways.'

'They knew well enough how to insult me!' said Adhelm. 'Why did they come here, only to insult me? What do they *want*?'

'Adhelm,' said Egwin. 'Listen to me. They came from the wood to see your hall – to see our gathering, to hear our music – it was innocent curiosity, merely. Before we speak or act hastily, let us consider if we may have – however unwittingly – insulted them?'

'Insult *them*?' The King sat straighter in his chair, and his face deepened another shade of red. 'By setting the tables with a feast? Giving them gold? Offering them my own blood – and all this to creatures that haven't a stitch to cover themselves with, nor so much as a bone pin to pin up their hair? No!' He smacked his hand on the arm of his chair. 'A man cannot allow another to spit on him and sneer at him – a King cannot allow his blood and his country to be spat on!'

Egwin spoke, but his words were lost in the rumble of assent from the crowd, in approving cheers. The old man sat still and waited until the noise had quietened. Then he raised his voice, which was thin and dry, but clear. Everyone heard. 'My Lord, if you were in a sound sleep, and the Thunderer woke you with the din of His chariot wheels and the glare of His thrown hammer, would you quarrel with Him? Would you denounce Him, and swear that you would be revenged on Him?'

The crowd fell silent. King Adhelm glowered, but was unable to think of anything to say until, at last, he burst out, 'That's different!'

'No, Adhelm, no. You would not dare to quarrel with the Thunderer because you know yourself, King as you are, to be a flea to Him. He may not notice your insolence, or He may choose to hunt you down and crack you between His fingernails, and you would not dare provoke Him.'

'Thunor has never come into my hall and insulted me to my face!' Adhelm said.

'He has pissed on you a thousand times,' the old man replied. 'The Wood Women are not the Thunderer, Adhelm, but they are of His kin. No man suffers an insult gladly, it is true – but a wise man –

and a King most of all – picks his quarrels carefully, and never fights except when he has a chance of winning.'

Kenelm studied his uncle. The King was still angry but his expression had turned baffled.

'There is no need for anyone to lose face,' Egwin said. 'It was a misunderstanding. Send word that you are sorry you were misunderstood – apologise for nothing more. You are sorry that you were misunderstood and you wish–'

'King, I must be heard!' The voice was cool and measured and rose clearly above all other noise in the hall. It was a woman's voice. Silence fell again, from the sheer astonishment of all there.

King Adhelm peered into the crowd of those gathered before his seat. 'Who spoke?'

'I did, King.' A woman came forward. Men – even athelings – stepped aside for her, in surprise. She made her way to the front of the gathering, stood before the king and looked him in the face. She had to tilt back her head to do it, since he was a big man, seated on a dais, and she was not a tall woman. It seemed she was a married woman, since her head was wrapped in a linen hood that revealed only her face. A long straight robe of uncoloured grey wool hung straight from her shoulders to her ankles. Below its hem could be seen strong leather boots. Around her middle was a belt of rope, from which hung a horn spoon and a small knife, such as anyone might carry. Her hands were folded in front of her, hidden in the sleeves of her robe. She looked meek. She did not sound it.

'What do you do here?' The King was understandably irritated by the interruption. 'Where is your husband?'

'In Heaven, King.'

Kenelm started. A woman, apparently married, dressed so poorly, yet speaking so arrogantly, and claiming that her husband was in heaven? He looked over his shoulder, to see how far away the door was. Behind him stood the Abbot, who nodded to him, as if in greeting. At either side of the Abbot were two big monks.

'Oh Gods,' Kenelm said.

In a low voice the Abbot said, 'Do not take the Lord's name in vain.' The two monks stepped forward, showing their willingness to hold Kenelm should he try to escape. Kenelm took one wild look round and then stood still. He could not be the cause of an uproar in the King's hall; it would be disgraceful. And what right did he have to fight or run away? He had been given to the monastery, and had always known that he would be taken back there.

'Your husband is where?' The King's face was reddening again.

The woman's cool voice said, 'I am married to Our Lord in Heaven, Jesus the Christ. I am your Abbess, who prays for you.'

The King's fists tightened on the arms of his chair, as if he would rise. '*Who*? Who let this woman in here? Who is she?'

Egwin leaned over from his chair. 'The Lady Abbess, King. From the monastery.' The King still didn't understand. 'The community of Christians, King,' Egwin insisted.

'Oh, the Christians!' the King said, and relaxed a little. 'Go away, woman. I have important things to discuss here. Whatever it is you're wittering on about, I'll see you later.'

The Abbess' voice rose again, saying calmly, 'King, I shall speak. It is the Wood Demons I must speak about.'

Old Egwin said, 'Demons, Lady? Demons?'

'Or evil spirits,' she said. 'Or bogles. Or whatever you please to call them.'

'These demons, Lady,' Egwin said, 'have lately saved us from the Foreigners.'

120

'And have lately insulted our King and us,' she said. 'If they seemed to help us, it was for reasons of their own, and not for any good. This Our Lord Our God has revealed to me.'

Old Egwin tutted in exasperation and turned his head away. King Adhelm said, 'I am a son of Woden, and He lets me in on these little secrets – yet I don't know what you're talking about, Lady.'

'Woden is no god,' she said. 'It is an evil spirit.'

There was a long, shocked silence. People held their breaths and looked to the King, to see what he would do. Some faces were horrified. Others, Kenelm saw, were gleeful.

The King, after a moment, chose to laugh. 'My father Woden must have His uses for you, Lady. Maybe He wants to amuse us. You!' To Kenelm's fright, the King threw out his arm, pointing, and pointed straight at him. 'I see you there!' Kenelm quaked. 'Come and take your woman home, before I lose my temper.'

'My Lord King–' said a voice directly behind Kenelm. It was the Abbot. The King was pointing at the Abbot, and hadn't even noticed Kenelm.

'Don't dicker with me! Come and take your woman home now!'

'King–' said the Abbess.

'My Lord King—' said the Abbot.

'And give her something to eat! And have something yourself! Like sticks, the pair of you. Minds don't work right without food, man, don't you know that? How can you work at all without food?'

'My Lord King, the Abbess rules me. I don't rule her.'

'Then be a man and stand up to her! Don't bring your tiddling hearth-side problems to me. Take her away out of my court!'

'King—'

'My Lord King—'

The gathered crowd of athelings and advisers laughed behind their hands, and pointed. The monks and the Abbot had drawn closer together, staring round at the sniggering people.

'King!' the Abbess cried. 'Since you will not hear the word of God, you will not – but a time will come, not so far distant, when you *will* listen!'

'Are you still jabbering, woman?'

'We came here in pursuit of *him*!' There was no doubt that the Abbess was pointing at Kenelm now. 'A runaway novice, gifted to our house by yourself!'

The King peered in Kenelm's direction, squinted

at his face for a moment, with an expression that mingled exasperation with bafflement, and then said, 'Oh it's *him*! That one! Which one is he, Egwin? – oh never mind! Boy, why didn't you go back to your place when you were told? Speak up!'

Kenelm had nothing to say. He knew that nothing he said would be accepted.

'Do you feed your apprentices as you feed yourselves, Lady?' the King asked. 'Feed them better and maybe they won't run away. Take him away and take yourselves out of my court! Get back to your own place and, please Woden, stay there!'

The Abbess bowed her linen-veiled head. 'I shall leave your presence, King. For now. I shall return.'

'Tcha!' the King said, and turned away from her. To Egwin he said. 'So tell me, how do we make our peace with the Wood Women?'

The Abbess came through the crowd towards Kenelm, her monks and her Abbot. Although people smirked as she passed, and grinned and stared, they stood aside for her, and she ignored them. As she reached him, the Abbot fell in behind her, following her to the hall door. The two monks took hold of Kenelm's arms and marched him away between them. He thought of fighting and running – but it would have meant an ignominious scene, and he would probably have lost in the end. Better, he thought, at least for now, to submit.

The Abbess led them through the streets of the Borough, through lanes where ladies strolled and servants ran on errands. Kenelm saw the main road that led to the gates, with carts being dragged along it, and the idea of escape rose in his mind again . . . But the King had acknowledged the Abbess's ownership of him. If he ran, she would raise a hue and cry, and he would soon be brought down and dragged back, like an escaped thrall. That was all he was, for all the fancy names and talk of God and holiness. He was a thrall, given away like a pig or a donkey, owned by the Abbess.

The Abbess led them through the door of one of the smaller, older halls. Another party of people were making themselves comfortable around a fire at its lower end, and they gawped as they passed, curious about the bizarre Christians. A curtain screened the upper end of the hall, and the Abbess drew aside a fold and led them behind it. Here, thrown down on the wall-benches, were the packs the monks had carried. Kenelm understood that some royal steward, receiving the Abbess' party, had made her standing with the King very clear. Not only had she been lodged in one of the lesser halls, but she hadn't even been given the whole of it for her own use. She had only the upper end, behind the curtain.

The Abbess seated herself on the wall bench and folded her hands in her lap. She said, 'Kenelm, come here. Stand in front of me.'

One of the monks gave him a shove, and Kenelm tottered a step or two, ending in front of her. She sat still for some long moments, looking cooly into his face. Then she said, 'You think you are still an atheling, and so you behave with all the arrogance of an atheling. But no. Your life as an atheling is over. You are a brother of our community now, and nothing more. A saved soul, one who will know eternal union with the one true God, but a humble soul all the same. One who must obey his Abbess.'

Kenelm could not deny this, so kept his head lowered and stayed silent; but he did not feel obedient.

'News was brought us of your doings,' the Abbess said. 'You have gone into the wood, they say.' She spoke with more difficulty and distaste as she went on. 'And spoken with. Danced with. The Wood Demons. Is this so?'

'I carried out the errand the King my uncle gave me,' Kenelm said.

'Your uncle! You have no uncle! You have no family

– except in Christ. I am your mother – your spiritual mother, and the Abbot is your father. Do you understand?'

It seemed to Kenelm that his mouth was plastered shut, so hard did he find it to unset his teeth and answer, 'Yes, Lady.'

'So you spoke with these Wood Demons?'

'I spoke with the Wood People, yes, Lady.'

'You spent days in the wood, we were told. You had. Dealings. With these creatures.'

'I was sick. They cared for me.'

The Abbess pursed her lips and nodded. 'And they had names, these creatures?'

Kenelm felt a faint prickling of alarm. To know a name gives power over the named. 'Why are you, Lady Abbess, interested in their names?'

From behind him came the Abbot's voice. 'It's not for you to question the Abbess!'

The Abbess allowed a pause, so that Kenelm would have time to feel guilt. 'I ask you again: What did they call themselves?'

Kenelm felt his backbone stiffening with atheling pride. Care for his uncle's honour half-persuaded him that he should obey these people, but it was becoming more than he could do. 'And I ask you again, Lady: Why do you wish to know their names?'

The Abbot tutted impatiently, but the Abbess held her hands high, signalling that they should have patience. She clasped her hands at her breast, just under the silver cross she wore. 'Brother Kenelm, a pedlar passed by our monastery and stayed the night with us, and he told us the tale of your adventures, as he had heard them told at court. As I listened a mood of black and cold despair came over me, to think that our land is full-filled with such lost and ungodly creatures, calling men and women to their destruction. With all my heart and soul I longed to save them and bring them into the shelter of the One True God's love. I knelt in my cell that night and wept and prayed for guidance, and God spoke to me very clearly, and told me that I must leave the safety and peace of the monastery and go into the wood – even into the pathless wood – and seek out these poor creatures and speak to them God's Spell. And when I bring them, tame, from the wood, singing God's praise, then many, many more will come to God.'

Behind Kenelm the Abbot muttered, 'God is good,' and the two monks echoed him.

The Abbess leaned towards Kenelm. 'I want you to help me in God's work. Tell me the names those creatures call themselves, so I can work on them

God's Spell and save them. You must tell me, Kenelm. You must.'

'Lady,' Kenelm said, 'what if the Wood Women do not want to hear the word of your God?'

'No creature can refuse to hear the Truth.'

Kenelm thought of the Wolf-Sisters, beautiful and naked under the leaf-light of the trees, their long hair loose about them. He thought of this grey-gowned nun, all trace of her hair covered by a linen cap, earnestly preaching at them. In his mind, he saw the sisters laughing, showing their sharp teeth.

He saw the sisters gathering about the monks and the Abbot, laughing at them, putting their arms round them and kissing their cheeks. It was a scene he would like to see.

'You are right, Lady,' he said. 'The truth should be heard. The Wood Women – Wood Demons, if you will – call themselves Wulfruna, Wulfgifu and Wulfgara – Wolf-Counsel, Wolf-Gift and Wolf-Spear. I will even guide you, if I can, to the spot where they appeared to me.'

The Abbess was surprised, but recovered herself. 'Very good, Brother Kenelm. You have deserved punishment but, when we return to the monastery, I shall remember that you were helpful.'

'Oh, thank you, Lady,' Kenelm said and, inside himself, laughed.

9

A crucifix

The Abbess stooped, breathing hard and pressing her hands to her chest. They had walked for miles, over rough ground full of humps and hollows that turned the feet and strained the knees and ankles. Gradually the forest's broad grassy rides had turned into the narrow, overgrown paths of the wood, and then even those paths had vanished. They bent and twisted and crouched to get under branches, and forced their way through undergrowth. Kenelm and the young monks were still fresh – they were used to hard work in the monastery's fields – but the Abbot was flagging. The Abbess, who had never laboured and who had for years piously denied herself food and rest, was nearing exhaustion.

The Abbot placed his hand under her elbow. 'We should rest, Lady.'

'No.' She drew breath painfully. 'No, we must go on. Kenelm, are we near?'

All around them were the arches and vaulting of the trees, the greens and golds and russets of the wood, and its deep silence. 'We are in the wood, Lady,' Kenelm said. 'If you call the demons, they will hear you.'

She pushed the Abbot away and gathered her robes about her, brushing leaves and dirt from their skirts. 'I shall summon them,' she said.

'But will they come?' Kenelm sat in the dry, coppery brown leaves beneath a large beech. He looked about at the burgeoning wood, the growth all around, and he felt, to the full, how much he hated the Abbess and her monastery – the greyness, the meanness, the poor food, the endless work, the deliberate refusal of comfort. He was eager to see her fail.

The Abbess dropped to her knees, clasped her hands and bowed her head. The Abbot knelt too; and then so did the monks.

'Lord Jesus, hear our prayer,' the Abbess said, and

the others muttered, 'Hear our prayer.'

'Lord Jesus, ever merciful and forgiving, hear our prayer that these poor, lost creatures, fettered by sin, may be pardoned by your loving kindness.'

'Hear our prayers,' the men repeated raggedly.

'Bring the Wood Demons to us, lead them to us, bring them here to us, Lord!'

'Bring them to us, Lord.'

'Holy Lord Jesus Christ, Who cast down the Devil into Hell, Who crushed that roaring lion, hasten to us here, who cry aloud for help, and snatch from the clutches of the noonday devil these poor, lost, ignorant things. Strike terror, Lord! Strike terror into the beast that lays waste your vineyard!'

'Oh yes!' cried the Abbot.

'Fill us, your servants, fill us with the courage to fight that reprobate dragon, who slavers for souls – fill us with courage and let him not despise us!'

'Courage, Lord!' the Abbot cried, throwing back his head, and one of the monks spread his arms wide to the trees and the sky above and shouted, 'Fill me with courage, Lord!'

'Let us face them, let them hear Your Word – may Your Words enter into their hearts and fill them with Your Spirit and let them be saved! Let them be saved!' The Abbess' voice was rising and travelling away through the arches of the trees, the veils of leaves.

'Oh Lord!' the Abbot cried, raising his arms above his head. 'Let them be saved.'

'Save them! Save them!' said the monks.

Kenelm, grinning, stretched himself out at full length in the dry leaves beneath the beech tree. The depths of the wood were still and untroubled. A leaf shifted in a slight breeze. Otherwise there was no sound; only the drowsy contentment of the trees.

Until the Abbess shrieked, 'Oh, aid us, aid us, Lord! Send us the Wood Demons! Wulfgara! Wulfgifu! Wulfruna! Send them to us. Save them, Lord, save them!'

'Save them! Save them!'

Kenelm sat up again. To speak a name aloud was to summon the one named – so he had always been told. Eagerly he searched for any sign of the Wolf-Sisters' approach – a rustling in the leaves, a parting of branches . . . There was nothing. He listened so hard that he caught the sound of a brook running somewhere in the distance, but nothing more.

The Abbess flung out her arms in the shape of a cross, lifting her face. She prayed, silently. The monks and the Abbot fell silent too, their shoulders hunched, their hands tightly clenched together in fervent prayer.

The silence, the kneeling, the praying, went on for a long time – half a day at least, it seemed to Kenelm. He listened to the breeze in the leaves, to the occasional burst of bird-song, to the distant rippling of water. Please come, he said to himself, silently. He didn't want the Christians to go back to the Royal Borough, proclaiming that the Wood Women had been afraid to face them.

'Dear God!' the Abbess cried out, at one point, startling him. The monks remained silent. Still there was no sign of the Wolf-Sisters.

Kenelm couldn't stand it. He was impatient to see them again, and he was bored. Getting to his feet, he reached above his head, took hold of the thickest twig he could put his hand to, and wrenched until he broke it.

'Why do you break our tree?'

It was a woman's voice, carrying through the silence of the wood. The Abbess raised her head. Kenelm turned this way and that, searching for the speaker but seeing no one.

· Close by there was a tread, and hanging curtains of leaves shivered and whispered as something brushed them and stirred them. A singing bird hushed. A glimpse of grey showed through the green and russet and Kenelm caught a whiff – a strong, rank whiff.

And then there were three wolves. They stood poised among the leaves. Their long, narrow heads were framed with manes of grey fur, their ears were pricked sharply, and their yellow-green eyes stared.

'Welcome!' cried the Abbess, before Kenelm could speak. She stretched her thin arms towards them. 'Welcome, sisters, in the name of Jesus the Christ, our Lord, our God! – Are these they, Kenelm, are these they?'

He tried to answer and found he could not speak. He nodded.

The Abbess turned back to the watching wolves. 'Sisters, sisters,' she said. Behind her, the monks had lifted their heads and were looking at the wolves with more apprehension – glancing at them sidelong, not daring to stare openly.

'Sisters, I have such good news to bring you, how can I begin? I have to tell you of the coming of this world's Lord – how He was born and the world was saved! I have to tell you how He died for us!' She pressed her hands to her breast and lifted her head to look at the leaves overhead. 'He died that we might live for ever!'

One of the wolves sat, and grinned, letting its tongue hang out of its mouth. Another half turned away, as if about to return to the depths of the wood.

'Listen, sisters!' The Abbess stretched out her arms. 'Sisters! Put on your woman-shapes – so you can hear my words! Listen as women, sisters, not as wild beasts! Oh, hear me, sisters!'

Kenelm was wondering if these were not, in fact, three wolves, but even as the thought crossed his mind, the seated wolf rose and continued to rise, stretching itself upwards. Its grey turned white – there was a fall of darkness about its head – and, instead of a wolf, a woman stood before them, a grey wolfskin hanging from her shoulders. A heavy, tangled fall of black hair fell down about her, hiding her breasts, but the small round of her belly, the fur of her groin, the curves of her thighs, were naked. The Abbot winced and lowered his head. The younger monks stared, their mouths open, before both blushed red. One turned his face away, the other hid his in his hands.

'Oh, sister! You are welcome!' said the Abbess. 'Speak to me – tell me your name!'

'Why are you in our wood? Why did you break our tree?' It was Wulfruna.

'It is Jesus' wood,' said the Abbess. 'All the world

is His creation. Come and sit with me – eat with me–' She glanced behind her and signalled at one of the monks, who pulled at a bag on his shoulder and opened it. 'Let me tell you about Jesus.'

'It is our wood,' Wulfruna said. 'My wood and my sisters' wood.'

The other two wolves rose, and stretched and turned, in the blink of an eye, to women. 'Kenelm! Have you come back to us?' That was Wulfgifu.

'He's brought a feast with him!' That was Wulfgara, looking at the monks.

'Here! Here!' said the Abbess. The monk was unpacking the bag he carried, and she was taking things from him and leaning forward to spread them on the leaf-covered ground. There was bread, and a lump of butter, and another of cheese, wrapped in large leaves. The monk passed her apples and a bundle of carrots, and the Abbess laid them beside the other food.

Wulfruna came forward, her sisters following. Their hair parted as they stepped, and their breasts bobbed into sight. 'We don't eat such stuff,' said Wulfruna, and kicked leaves over the food as she passed. She went on, past the monks who could not look at her, to Kenelm, and Wulfgara and Wulfgifu went with her.

'Is there news of Egwin?' 'Gifu took his arm and pressed herself to his side.

Kenelm felt laughter rising up inside him, unstoppably, from the sheer pleasure of being near them again. He trembled with it. 'He sends you thanks and love.' He could hardly speak the words.

'Why have you brought these here?' 'Gara asked.

'They begged me to guide them here! They want to preach to you and conquer you.' He laughed, the noise loud in a wood that had fallen silent. 'I want to see you conquer them.'

All three of the Wolf-Sisters looked over their shoulders at the Abbess with their long, intent stares. They had the stillness of alert animals, the stillness that shifts so quickly into flight or attack.

The Abbess withstood their eyes, her fists clenched at her sides, but Kenelm saw a fleeting expression cross her face. It might have been fear. It might only have been a realisation of what had answered her call. 'In the name of Jesu the Christ,' she said, 'listen to me! Listen to your salvation, sisters!'

Wulfruna left Kenelm and went to the Abbess. Her sisters followed. Kenelm felt laughter overcoming him again.

The Wolf-Sisters reached for the Abbess as they neared her. They were taller than she, and more strongly made, and naked, and they smelled of sweat and earth. Kenelm, shaking with laughter, saw the Abbess hold herself from stepping back, away from them.

'What have you come to tell us, little woman?' Wulfruna asked, crooningly, as she touched the Abbess' linen headdress. 'That the earth dies every year and comes again in Spring? We live in the wood; we know.'

'Don't you have hair?' Wulfgara asked.

They pulled at the Abbess' headdress, trying to withdraw the pins. The Abbess stood tall and straight, ignoring them, but their fingers were insistent, and soon she put up her hands to push theirs away. They were quicker and stronger; their hands evaded the Abbess' and plucked and tugged at the headdress.

'Stop, stop!' the Abbess said.

The Abbot and one of the monks started forward but Wulfgifu – gentle 'Gifu – whipped round her head and glared and snarled. The men stopped short.

Kenelm called out, 'What – are you afraid of women? Won't your God protect you from them?' It was ignoble, this name-calling, and he knew it, but the glee he felt wouldn't let him stay quiet.

'Runa and 'Gara, despite the Abbess' protests and

struggles, pulled out the pins that held her headdress, and tugged it from her head. Beneath it the Abbess' skull was knobbly, the fine grey hair cropped so short that her white scalp shone through it. The Wolf-Sisters laughed: fierce, barking laughs.

Dropping to her knees, the Abbess put her hands together. Raising both her hands and her face, she shouted to the sky. 'I conjure you, ancient serpent, by the Judge of the Living and the Dead, by your Creator, by the Creator of the Whole Universe, by Him who has the power to throw you into Hell, to depart from here, in fear, in trembling—'

Wulfgara, laughing, seized her at the shoulder by a handful of loose gown and dragged her sideways, throwing her full length on the ground. Wulfruna stepped to straddle the woman with a swift, crouching motion that sent a jolt of excitement and dread through Kenelm. It reminded him of a greyhound lunging for a hare, of a cat pouncing for a mouse. He opened his mouth to shout but stopped, horrified, when he realised that the words on his tongue were, 'Kill her!' He gasped and said, almost in a whisper, 'Leave her!'

He knew it was what he should say. He disliked the Abbess, but she was a woman, and an ageing one. She was due his protection. Still his heart was fierce inside him, and the words, 'Kill her!' still rang in his head. 'Leave her!'

Wulfgara turned and, at her look, he stopped, as struck with cowardice as the Christians. 'Gara had frozen, but there was a tautness to her stillness that threatened, speaking of strength and suddenness. In her glittering, glaring eyes and her drawn-back lips was a ferocity that made the hair prickle on his body and brought sweat from under his arms. He was filled with shame that he had not spoken as he wished, but still he could not bring himself to say those words.

Seeing that Kenelm did not dare come closer, Wulfgara relaxed and laughed. She threw up her head, throwing back her thick fell of dark hair and, in so doing, her eyes fell on the Abbot and the monks. With another laugh she left the Abbess and sauntered towards them. 'Runa and 'Gifu, seeing her intention, followed her.

The Abbess, left alone, struggled to her knees. She tried to twist round as she did so, to see what was happening to her monks, and overbalanced, tangled in her robes. She fell heavily, with a groan of expelled breath. Kenelm watched, knowing he should help her, but hating her too. He wished her dead, and denied that he wished it. He could not move a step.

The Wolf-Sisters smiled as they sashayed towards the monks, hips swaying, and long falls of hair swinging to cover and uncover bobbing breasts. The Abbot raised his arm to fend them off and, when they still came, he hastily fell back behind the young monks, who were appalled and didn't know whether to stand or run.

The sisters laughed, and spread out to encircle the monks and drive them together. Wulfruna stretched out her arms. 'What big hands we have!'

'What big eyes!' said Wulfgifu.

'And what big teeth we have!' said Wulfgara.

One of the monks bravely came forward, holding his wooden crucifix before him, but Wulfruna snarled and sprang at him, and he faltered and ran away, crashing through greenery, tripping on a briar and almost falling before catching himself.

A long, joyous laugh rose from the sisters, and they abruptly abandoned the chase, turned on their heels and came back for the Abbess. Wolves pick out the weakest of the herd. The monks stood huddled together at a distance, peering through the leaves, watching as a herd often watches its weakest member taken. Kenelm could hear their prayers, and he started to laugh again.

The Wolf-Sisters closed on the Abbess. They were

not threatening – except that their faces were full of the intentness with which a cat watches a bird it means to kill, and their bodies moved with the same slow, controlled strength and purpose. Kenelm was shaken by an eagerness to see them spring and kill – he shook with it. It was the same excitement and eagerness he remembered from the hunt. The whisper in his head said, 'Kill her! Kill her!'

The old woman, with great effort, got herself to her feet and turned to face them, though Kenelm could see her trembling. It was her courage that struck through to him. Even so, he had to struggle against more powerful feelings before he could unclench his teeth and say, through a constricted throat, 'Leave her.'

Wulfruna's intent stare shifted to him, and her eyes shoved him away. The fear that came on him at her look was more than fear of attack, more than fear of teeth and claws. It was fear of the whole wood: of its vast tracklessness and age, of its silence and darkness. He felt his muscles tensing and bending him into a crouch, pushing him, driving him round the Abbess and the sisters in a crouch, his fingers hooking. He was afraid of the wood and he was afraid of himself.

The Abbess stood still as the Wolf-Sisters encircled

her, holding her crucifix before her. The almost-bald scalp covering her knobbly head moved as she gulped. She said, half-pleading, 'Listen to me! Listen! Be saved!'

Reaching out, Wulfruna pulled at a wisp of grey hair. 'From what will you save us?'

'From damnation!'

The sisters looked at each other, with no understanding.

'From death of the soul and never-ending torment!' said the Abbess. Raising her arms, she took the silver crucifix from about her neck. 'Will you hear the word of the new God? Will you?'

'New God?' said Wulfgifu.

Wulfruna said, 'There are no new Gods. There are only the Gods that always were and always will be.' She crouched swiftly to speak into the Abbess' ear and then passed on, circling her. 'And we are of their kin!'

'Demons!' said the Abbess.

They circled her. 'Demons, spooks and bogles,' 'Runa said. She put out her hand as if to gently touch the Abbess' head, but hooked her fingers, and when she withdrew her hand, she left stripes of red on the Abbess scalp.

The Abbess held her crucifix in her hand by its

lower stem. Her other hand closed on its upper stem. Kenelm saw clearly. The Abbess drew one hand away from the other, and from the crucifix emerged a shining silver blade. And then Wulfgifu – beautiful, gentle 'Gifu – stepped between him and the Abbess.

He did not see the Abbess move, but he saw Gifu stumble back and fall. He saw the Abbess fall to her knees above her, and raise her arm and stab and stab.

'Almighty God!' said the Abbess, gasping from effort. 'Defend us! In the battle. Against the powers. Of darkness. Lord of Peace! Cast down Satan. Under. Our feet . . .'

Kenelm stood appalled, transfixed. Wulfgifu writhed, arching her back, twisting – she twisted from a woman into a wolf and made to crawl away, but the Abbess struck at her again. 'Gifu howled.

'Stop, in Woden's name!' Kenelm yelled.

The Abbess looked at him, on her knees, her face blank and astonished. In her raised hand she held the bladed crucifix, its silver running with blood.

'Gifu crawled away, a wolf, but she shuddered and panted. Kenelm raised his eyes and looked beyond her and saw Wulfruna and Wulfgara. In the same instant their eyes met his, and he felt death touch him – and then 'Gara and 'Runa were gone –

whether in wolf- or woman-shape he couldn't tell.

'Gifu was stretched on the ground, a great long wolf with grey and tawny fur. He went to her, knelt beside her, and felt the wet, bloodied fur of her chest, feeling for the heart beating under the ribs. She twisted, and the wolf-fur parted and fell apart, showing the woman sprawled inside it. Under Kenelm's hand, the heart-beat raced, stuttered, and stopped.

He raised his head and looked at the Abbess. He had no word to say, but felt his lips stretch back over his teeth.

Behind him he heard the trampling as the monks and the Abbot hastily drew near, afraid of the wolves who had fled into the wood.

The Abbess shifted from her knees to sit on the grass. She passed her bloodied crucifix to a monk, to clean for her. 'Silver,' she said. 'The Holy Virgin's metal. Taken from the altar – quenched in a font of holy water – blessed by the Saved. It has brought peace to one who . . . ran on more feet than she should.'

All Kenelm's laughter and glee had turned to rage that shook him and choked him. Spluttering, tears spurting from his eyes, he yelled, 'Brought peace?'

'Peace and eternal rest in God's love. Oh Great

Lord Jesus, we beg you to keep the evil spirit from further molesting these servants of yours. May your goodness and peace, oh Jesus, take possession of this poor creature; and may we no longer fear any evil, since You are with us, Amen.'

'Amen,' said the Abbot and the monks, their voices gruff and shaking.

The Abbess looked up at them. 'We will take the body back with us. To show the people.'

Kenelm stood above the body. He was so angry that he was unsteady and staggered. 'Lady,' he said. 'Lady.' He couldn't find enough breath.

Around them the wood was utterly still. Not a bird twittered, not a leaf moved.

'Lady,' Kenelm said. 'Listen to the wood. You will never leave it.'

10

Hunting

'We walk with God,' the Abbess said. ' "Yea, though we walk through the valley of the shadow of death, we will fear no evil, for He is with us, His rod and His staff they comfort us." '

The rage thrumming through Kenelm, choking him, shaking him, gathered itself together in one outcry. With all his strength he threw himself at the Abbess, to rip off her face, to tear her open—

The monks who had been afraid of the Wood Women were not afraid of Kenelm, and blocked him with their bodies. He tried to go through them, hardly noticing they were there, but was flung backwards to fall, sprawling, in the wood's undergrowth, his ears filled with the noise of leaves crushing and twigs breaking. Winded, breathless, he scrambled up at once – but saw the monks drawing together and pressing back, their eyes intent on something behind him. Kenelm snapped round his head to look.

Out from the leaves stepped a tall, naked woman, her dark hair hanging about her. Wulfruna.

Wulfgara emerged from the leaves, as if made of broken sunlight and leaf-shade.

Pacing through the bushes and flowers, grass and leaves, passing through light and shade, they moved towards the Abbot and the monks. The man holding the Abbess' knife raised it threateningly, but the Wood Women came on and the monks fell back, one stumbling on the outstretched arm of Wulfgifu's corpse. Step by step, they retreated further. Behind them, the Abbot supported the Abbess.

As soon as they had been driven back from Wulfgifu's body, 'Runa made a sweeping stoop and snatched up the wolfskin, dragging it free. Turning on her heel, she brought it to Kenelm.

He was on his feet, fists clenched at his side. He breathed hard, rage still hot inside him, looking for his chance. As 'Runa halted in front of him, he looked into her face, and her long dark eyes. Holding his gaze, she raised the heavy wolfskin and put it round his shoulders. Lifting her arms high, she raised the wolf's head and set the mask on top of his head. Leaning forward, her hands on his chest, she kissed him on the mouth, and then drew back, smiling.

The wolfskin tightened across Kenelm's shoulders, creeping about his arms, pressing to his spine. Grey fur thickened along his arms. A heart's beat of alarm was swept away by exhilaration. The skin wrapped him round, tightly and completely, and his muscles stretched and pulled, as if with hard labour. His heart beat with a greater thump and swell. His bones were as strong and solid as iron bars. Strength vibrated through him.

He lashed his tail against his sides, feeling it thump his flanks, feeling the lithe movement uncoil down a spine as strong and flexible as a young branch. He growled, his lips sliding over long teeth, and the sound shivered in the depths of his chest, grating in his throat, resounding in his skull.

There was a stink – a stink that reached down into his lungs – a greasy, smoky, musky stink, a smell of men. And there were the men, and the woman, the monks and the Abbess. There they were, going from him, step by step, crouching with fear, wanting to run but afraid.

Their fear made the hair rise along his spine. Their creeping, fearful movements tugged him after them as surely as if they pulled him on a rope. Easy prey! The growl thrummed through him again, his muscles gathered, his heart pumped, and he launched himself. Streaks of grey beside him were his sisters. Grass and twigs parted before them, thrashing in their wake.

The monks, the Abbess, stretched their legs and ran – the Abbot hauling the Abbess by the arm – ran – crashing through breaking bushes, tearing themselves from thorns.

In powerful, bounding strides, the wolves followed. It was like flying – there was hardly a sense of effort, only of the pleasure of the body stretching, the muscles gathering, the glad jolt of meeting the rebounding turf. The moaning, fleeing prey were overtaken and turned back, herded together so they jostled each other and struck out and yelled in terror and frustration.

Wulfruna and Wulfgara came arrowing through the cover of leaves, darting with open mouths and bared teeth. One monk ran into a tree and, crying out, fell down. The other floundered through nettles.

The Abbot, parted from his Abbess, lay on his back and called out in despair. Wulfgara silenced him.

Wolf-Kenelm saw the Abbess, tottering, looking about her, clutching at a tree to keep her feet. Crouching low, he stalked her, his eyes fixed on her. She saw him and, with weakened, fluttering movements, tried to escape him. Advancing pace by crouching pace, he drove her before him.

Gasping hard for breath, she tried to run, tripped on her robe, caught herself, clutched up her skirts and stumbled on, failing, from exhaustion and fear. Twice she turned and tried to face him, but the black lips and hot red mouth, the long teeth, the slitted, blazing yellow eyes must all have been, to her, a vision of Satan, and she could not stand against it. Unable to shriek, for lack of breath, she scrambled on, hauling herself with desperate hands from tree to tree, rattling leaves and branches.

As Kenelm followed her, so slowly, he could feel the strength in his tensed muscles. His nose and mouth were full of her smell and taste. His teeth chattered, his jaw trembled with the eagerness to seize and bite, until he could not be patient any longer. He sprang, closed his teeth about her scrawny thigh, driving his fangs through woollen robe and flesh with all the strength of wolf-jaws, locked about her bones in the unbreakable wolf-bite. An extraordinary thrill went through him, prickling in his hair. This was life. He set his feet, wrenched with his shoulders, his neck, his spine, and wrenched his prey from her feet. Using that strength felt better than had anything in his life. The blood in his mouth was better, richer than any food.

He shook her, he dragged her through the herbage and low growth, breaking twigs, crushing grass, while she shrilled mindlessly in pain and fear. Letting go her leg, he trod over her, pressing her down, and closed his jaws on her throat.

Wulfgara left the Abbot and joined her sister in tormenting the monk who had run into the tree. He had scrambled up, but couldn't run, for Wulfruna had his habit in her teeth. She let him go when 'Gara came up, and they harried the monk between them, springing at him, snarling, now from one side, now the other, so that he spun and turned, jumping back from the jaws. When he was frantic and almost senseless with panic, Wulfruna leapt at him, striking him in the chest, and knocked him down. Wulfgara was on him at once, choking him.

They left his body and were away together, coursing through the wood, on the last monk's trail. His scent was in their noses, and they could hear him, stumbling and crashing and panting. For a long time they played with him, appearing as he splashed through the stream, snarling at him from one bank so that he slipped on the stream's pebbles and wallowed on hands and knees back towards the other side – but as soon as he reached it, the other wolf would appear, turning him back.

He tried to make his way down the stream, and the wolves came into the water after him, driving him up the soft earth of the bank, panting, digging at the leaf-litter, his face coated in sweat. He was almost at the top when a wolf appeared above him, grinning down at him, sending him slithering down to the water again.

He knelt in the stream and prayed for salvation. Wulfgara leapt on his back, sending him sprawling. Wulfruna locked her teeth in his throat and dragged him, struggling, out of the water. She kept her teeth clenched until he died. Before then, 'Gara had already begun to eat.

They ate, ripping and gulping; they gorged; and then they dragged themselves up the bank and lay down in the shelter of some hazel bushes. There they licked each other clean of blood, and raised a song for 'Gifu that silenced the wood. In the silence they slept.

Waking in the dawn dusk, they trotted back through the wood, following the scent, until they came to where Kenelm was sleeping, a long grey wolf, beside what remained of his meal. They slipped off their wolfskins and appeared as women. Kneeling beside him, they prodded him and laughed.

He woke and sat, the wolfskin slipping from him. The first thing he saw, in the clear light filtering through the trees, was what lay beside him: the mauled remains of the Abbess, bloodied and torn. Eaten.

'Gara and 'Runa crouched beside him. 'Gara put her hand on his shoulder. 'Runa stroked his hair.

In his mouth and throat was a thick, stale taste, of blood. His tongue was coated with fat and, between his teeth were shreds of meat. The wolfskin he wore was bloodied, the paws and chest and muzzle stained, the fur caked and dried into spikes.

'Shall you stay with us, then?' 'Gara asked.

'Wear 'Gifu's skin,' said 'Runa.

He started to his feet, throwing the skin away from him. His belly was heavy with meat and, unsteady, he staggered and almost stepped into the cavity of the body. He jumped away from it, loathing it. Spitting and wiping his mouth, he tried to rid of what was smeared there. He retched, but could not be sick.

The Wolf-Sisters rose to their feet and watched him. 'Shall you stay?' said 'Runa.

He shook his head; he shook his whole body in denial. Turning, he looked about, seeing only trees and narrow trails that lost themselves among leaves. No way seemed better than any other.

'If you go back to your own,' 'Runa said, 'we shall follow.'

Kenelm could only shake his head. He backed from them, turned, and went into the trees.

11

The end of the story

It was late in Aelfric's hall. Some candles had burned out; many were low and guttering. Darkness was thickening in the corners and among the rafters. The fires, too, had burned down, and the servants were reluctant to build them up again so late. Cold draughts were making themselves felt, and people were rubbing their arms, or drawing nearer to the fires.

But, if people had been growing sleepy and propping heavy heads on hands, now they were awake again and listening. They leaned to each other and whispered, their eyes on Kenelm even as they spoke.

At the high table, where Kenelm sat, people had drawn away from him on either side, leaving him alone in the red light of a dying torch that burned near him. It was as if they could still smell the blood on him.

'Here he is, then,' Kenelm said. 'Kenelm, come back from the wood. It's the end of his story.'

A silence fell. The darkness deepened as another candle, and another, went out. The ashes fell in the fires, and birds shifted and twittered in the thatch. From everywhere about the hall came soft whisperings as people spoke to their neighbours, but no one dared to speak aloud.

Aelfric leaned along the high table towards his guest and said, loudly enough for everyone to hear, 'But the story isn't ended. How did you – how did Kenelm Atheling leave the wood?'

'Hard travel. Following one trail until it ended, pushing through thorns and branches until he came on another; going by hill, by valley, by brook, by stone . . . And every step they were with him, saying, 'Come, live with us.' Saying, 'Wear the skin and be one of us.' 'We are two now,' they said, 'and once we were three – why will you leave us?' But – stay with them? When every night he lay beneath a tree and listened for their singing after they had killed and eaten. He had no hunger, no need to eat. He had a bellyful. When they came near him, he couldn't look at them.

'He came out of the wood at last and into the forest. He thought the going would be easier and quicker then, but – the wood followed him.'

Aelfric said, 'The wood followed?'

'With a noise like rushing water. Stems of briar thrusting themselves through grass and bush, clawing, grasping . . . Ivy rushing across rides and swarming up trees. Nuts falling to earth, and cracking and shoving down roots, sending up sprouts. An uprush of close-grown branches twisting themselves together, rustling of leaves opening . . . The earth shifting and falling as trees lifted their roots and walked . . . Kenelm looked behind him and saw the open forest ways closing as the wood came in – and from the edges of the marching wood came the wolves, flitting in and out, calling the wood on. He knew then that he would lead the wood to the doors of the Royal Borough – but where else had he to go?

'He saw people – herders and coppicers – but none would stop to speak to him. They heard the wood coming. They looked and saw it coming. And they saw Kenelm himself, draped in the bloody wolfskin that had been hung on him, bearded, ragged, dirty, gaunt – they saw him coming with the wood, and they ran.

'The wood swallowed fields. The ploughed strips, the banks and ditches were swarmed over by violets and wood sorrel, by dark-green nettles. Then came the saplings and the bushes and, as they claimed their ground and thickened, in came the snaring briars and honeysuckle.

'A village was taken by the wood. The saplings rooted in the street; the roots of bushes forced aside the stones of walls. Doorways were barred by holly, and the flimsy walls of huts shouldered aside by spreading trees. A bear stopped to drink at the village pool. The people had long since run away.

'Kenelm's uncle, King Guthlac, rode out to meet the wood. Kenelm saw him coming, on horseback, with a party of armed men and curious courtiers. They reined in their horses and sat watching the marching wood, their faces afraid and baffled.

'When Kenelm came close, the King stared at him a long time before he knew him, and even then he stared in horror or disgust at the wolfskin. "What is this?" the King demanded. "How is this happening? Why?"

'Kenelm shrugged. He had no words or strength

to explain. Turning, he looked to where the wood came on, with a whispering of leaves and stems, thinking he might see the wolves and point to them, but there was no sight of them. He shrugged again.

'The King stood in his stirrups and yelled at the wood. "Go back!" His voice spread out among the green shadows of the trees, died and faded. Nothing answered, but the wood came on.

' "Is this because I thanked you?" the King yelled. "Is this because I did you honour?"

'Kenelm trudged on, the heavy wolfskin patting at his back as he went, leaving the King and his company behind. Not even a bird's whistle answered the King's yells, but, behind him, Kenelm could hear the wood walking.'

Aelfric said, 'Where is King Guthlac?'

'In the wood,' said Kenelm. 'Or his bones are. It's all wood now, that land. There are no fields, no villages, no boroughs – the wood has taken them back. On his way here, Kenelm came by his monastery – broken walls in the wood. So he came on, always trying not to hear their calls – and then, one day, the wood no longer followed.'

'Why?' Aelfric asked. 'How did you – did Kenelm – stop it?'

'He did nothing. The wood stopped. A day's walk

from here – you may go and look at it. Why have they stopped? Who can tell? Maybe they are tired of Kenelm and have gone to chase other meat. Kenelm walked on and that brought him here. And he brings you the news.'

Aelfric nodded. 'For that we thank him.' He paused and drummed his fingers lightly on the table. More candles had died, and the hall was darker still. 'What will he do now? Where will he go?'

Kenelm turned his head and looked into Aelfric's eyes. 'He thought to stay here.'

From the body of the hall came a gasp, a soft rustling as many people shifted and exclaimed. For a second, Aelfric looked away. Then he looked as steadily into Kenelm's eyes as Kenelm looked into his. 'We don't want you here.'

Kenelm, who had more than half-expected this answer, gave a tight, painful grin. He looked down the shadowed length of the hall, at the darkness where the candles had gone out, and the patches of warm light where they still burned. Pale smudges of faces looked back at him. 'Is there anywhere, do you think, where he would be welcome?'

Aelfric gave it a few moments' thought, then said honestly, 'No. Nowhere.'

Kenelm reached out and touched the drinking-horn that lay on the table. He looked up at the hangings round the walls, whose colours and patterns were sinking into darkness as the candles died. 'Do you think,' he said, 'that a wolf feels sorrow for what it has done?'

'No,' Aelfric said. 'None.'

Standing, Kenelm lifted the heavy wolfskin from the back of his chair, and raised it over his head. He stood like that for a moment, looking up into the rafters and the thatch, looking about at this small, homely hall, the last he would ever see. Then he set the toothed mask on top of his head, and let the forepaws dangle over his shoulders and chest.

A torch went out in one corner, and candles guttered. From the sway and flicker of darkness, of light, leapt a wolf – leapt, a grey streak, over the high table and landed on the floor before it as people started up with cries.

Straight through the dying fire the wolf ran, sending the flames and darkness spinning, scattering ash and embers, shifting the smoke skeins. Down the hall in great bounds as people clambered backwards over benches, carrying with it the stink of singeing and of wolf.

Aelfric, rising, bellowed, 'Open the doors!' and one man hurried to throw the hall door open wide.

Out went the wolf, into the darkness.

The people stood amazed in the darkening hall, as more candles blew out, as it grew colder, until they heard, far off, the singing of wolves.

Then they shut and barred the hall doors, built up the fires, relit the torches, and stayed there together, until daybreak.

THE BONE-DOG

Susan Price

Sarah has the perfect pet. She doesn't need to feed or exercise it. The bone-dog does everything she asks.

Even the bad things.

And Sarah begins to enjoy her new-found power . . .

HAUNTINGS

Susan Price

'Why?' I said. 'Why does she come back?'
Gran said: 'Why was her murdered, poor wench?'
Take it from me, that's what they're like, real
hauntings. All it takes to bring you to your knees
in suffocating fear is the sound of walking and
the jingle of a bunch of keys.

Ten terrifying hauntings that will linger in
your mind long after, that will make you
glance over your shoulder, that will fill you
with delicious unease . . . These are some of
the best ghost stories you will ever read.

NIGHTCOMERS

Susan Price

Last night I dreamed that I saw him crawling towards me on his hands and knees, though his eyes stared through me, as if he would crawl through me – and I woke in a cold horror that I could not explain and cannot forget . . .

A graveside lament, a stolen kiss, a lover's revenge, a mourner mute with grief . . .

Nine nerve-tingling night-time visitations to freeze your body and haunt your mind – an unforgettable collection of ghost stories by the author of the Carnegie Medal-winning *Ghost Drum*.

THE STORY-COLLECTOR

Susan Price

'Elsie, do you know any other stories?'
'Stories, Master?'
'Yes, you were telling one the other day in the kitchen, about a woman and the Devil.'
Elsie, with a thrill, sat down on one of the big polished chairs.
Mr Grimsby sat back in his chair and lifted his glass.
'Do begin.'
'Well, Master, it was like this . . .' Elsie said.

And so the Story-Collector gathers his stories, from housemaids and soldiers, from dogs and the dying – tales of all kinds and about all things. There's a tale of a dancing shilling, a soldier who died too soon, three husbands humiliated, a stingy old man, a king subdued and a dog who told lies . . .